P9-CBM-424

# FRiENDS

BY KRISTEN GUDSNUK

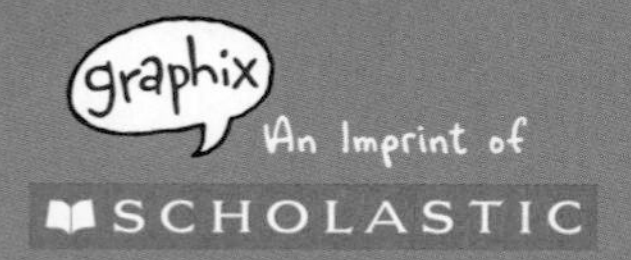

Library of Congress Control Number: 2017953347

ISBN 978-1-338-13922-8 (hardcover)
ISBN 978-1-338-13921-1 (paperback)

10 9 8 7 6 5 4 3 2 1 18 19 20 21 22

Printed in China 62
First edition, August 2018
Edited by Adam Rau
Book design by Phil Falco
Creative Director: David Saylor

To Penny.

GREAT-AUNT ELMA'S WILL JUST SAID: "THE FAMILY CAN SORT THROUGH MY STUFF."
82
WITKOWSKI

"HEAVEN KNOWS I HAVE ENOUGH OF IT TO GO AROUND."

NO, I WANT THE MAHOGANY ARMOIRE! IT MATCHES MY HOUSE!

SHE MUST HAVE KNOWN THE CHAOS THAT WOULD ENSUE.

I THINK I WOULD HAVE LIKED ELMA.
SHE CERTAINLY HAD A LOT OF FUN STUFF.

THIS VASE IS A **REPLICA** MING DYNASTY.

**ACTUALLY**, LINDA, WHY DON'T **YOU** TAKE THE VASE.
Pat pat

Flip Flip
Sketchbooks
HANDLE with CARE

PROPERTY OF
Elma Witkowski
SKETCHBOOK
SKETCHBOOK
PROPERTY OF
Elma Witkowski
ELMA WAS A PRETTY GREAT ARTIST.
MOM, CAN I KEEP THESE SKETCHBOOKS? THEY'RE REALLY COOL.
SURE, DANIELLE—
--LET **ME** SEE THOSE.
**I** WANT THEM. I LOVE ART.

YOU DON'T HAVE **ROOM** FOR THEM IN YOUR **HOUSE.**
OH, I DON'T HAVE **ROOM** FOR SOME **SKETCHBOOKS?**

TRACY, YOU'RE **UNBELIEVABLE.**
sketchbooks
HANDLE WITH CARE

**I'M** TAKING **HALF.**
**FINE.**
...

AUNT TRACY AND UNCLE DAVE TOOK ALL THE GOOD ONES.
DON'T EVEN **BOTHER** WITH THEM.

WHAT'S IN THE BOOK?
JUST... RANDOM STUFF. A LOT OF BLANK PAGES.

THERE'S A LITTLE STILL LIFE OF THAT LAMP AUNT TRACY TOOK.

...OF COURSE, WE'VE GOTTA SELL THE HOUSE.
HOW ARE WE GOING TO SPLIT THE MONEY?

I NEED THE MONEY MORE THAN YOU DO, TRACY.

WHY NOT SPLIT IT EVENLY?
AUNTIE ELMA ALWAYS LIKED ME BEST.

THEY'RE SO LAME. IT'S ALL JUST STUFF.
I DON'T KNOW WHY THEY CARE ABOUT LAMPS AND DRESSERS SO MUCH.

MAYBE YOU'D UNDERSTAND IF YOUR MOTHER HAD TAUGHT YOU THE VALUE OF MONEY. LAUREN.

YOINK!
I WAS READING THAT!

UGH. WHY DON'T YOU GO FIGHT UNCLE DAVE FOR A TOASTER.
TEENAGERS.

YOU KIDS WON'T TAKE CARE OF ANY OF THIS STUFF--

CRASH!

LOOK AT WHAT YOU'VE DONE!
CASE IN POINT.
CAN'T YOU CONTROL YOUR CHILD, DAVE?
WASN'T ME.

GO TO TIME-OUT!
WAH H Hh
Sigh...

blah blah blah
HERSTORY
THERE IS NO I in HONESTY

LIFE WAS SO MUCH EASIER IN SIXTH GRADE.
ha ha
SOLAR SISTERS
I HAD JOAN AND LEAH.
SOLAR SISTERS
I KNEW WHERE I BELONGED.

12:30 PM!

10:00 AM

12:30 PM

1 PM

LUCKILY THERE'S NO **RECESS** ANYMORE, BECAUSE I'D HAVE NO ONE TO PLAY WITH.
BATTLEM

YOU KNOW, IF YOU GAZE HARD ENOUGH INTO YOUR **LOCKER**, YOU'LL UNLOCK THE **MYSTERIES** OF THE **UNIVERSE.**

YOU SHOULD UNLOCK THE MYSTERIES OF YOUR **FACE!**

WOW, THAT CUT **DEEP.**

I CAN'T REMEMBER MY STUPID **SCHEDULE.**

Schedule
IT'S TAPED TO YOUR LOCKER.

IT'S **WOODWORKING.** I'M IN YOUR CLASS.

B RIIN GG

AAAAAAND WE'RE **LATE.**
FWOOSH!
GAHH!

WHY... THE HECK...
DO THEY... WANT TWELVE-YEAR-OLDS PLAYING WITH BAND SAWS, ANYWAY...?
THUM
IT'S PART OF A GOVERNMENT CONSPIRACY TO...
UM THUM THUM
PREPARE UPCOMING GENERATIONS... FOR SURVIVAL IN A TECHNOLOGY-FREE DYSTOPIA.
THUM THUM
I READ ABOUT IT ONLINE.

THAT'S THOUGHTFUL OF THEM.
huff
huff

MAYBE HE HASN'T TAKEN ATTENDANCE YET--

TOM TORRES, ONE MORE TARDY AND WE'RE SENDING A NOTE HOME TO YOUR PARENTS.
huff
huff
IF YOU BUILD IT
THEY WILL COME
PUSH

UNDERSTAND?

AND YOU, UM, WHAT'S YOUR NAME... YOU'RE TARDY TOO.
"what's your name"

BRRRING!
MIDDLE SCHOOL

SCHOOL BUS
MELTON SCHOOL DISTRICT

SUNNYSIDERS STAND TOGETHER!
WE ARE THE TEAM THAT'S OUT TO WIN!

GUYS, YOU'RE--YOU'RE EMBARRASSING ME! WE'RE NOT IN ELEMENTARY SCHOOL ANYMORE.

WE'RE NOT?!
I HAD ABSOLUTELY NO IDEA!

LEAH, ONCE YOU'RE A SUNNYSIDER, YOU'RE A SUNNYSIDER TILL YOU DIE. IT'S IN YOUR BLOOD.
I'M A MELTON MIDDLE SCHOOLER.

I'M NOT. MIDDLE SCHOOL SUCKS.
POKE POKE

IF ONLY YOU WERE IN CLUSTER I! YOU COULD MEET RHONDA! SHE'S AN AMAZING ARTIST.

LOOK WHAT SHE DID TO OUR ARMS.

IT REALLY STINKS THAT YOU'RE NOT EVEN IN OUR **LUNCHWAVE.**
I THINK YOU'D REALLY LIKE RHONDA.

Hey Melissa!
JOAN! LEAH! HEY! I FORGOT TO TELL YOU, MR. MAYLE--

OH, UH, HE'S OUR **MATH** TEACHER--HE'S ALWAYS GOT **CHALK** ON HIS FOREHEAD--

WELL, ANYWAY, SO JACOB IS JUST BEING BLAH BLAH BLAH BLAH

BYE, GUYS...
**BYE, DANY!!**

I THOUGHT YOU WERE TALKING TO A **BOY!** NO OFFENSE!
DANY'S A **GIRL!**

VROOOM

PAT PAT
THWOOP!

I WILL TAKE OVER THE EARTH, AS IS MY BIRTHRIGHT, AND MAKE YOU MY **QUEEN!**
**NEVER!!!**
WHEN WILL YOU REALIZE?
HUMANITY IS FOR **FOOLS!**
PRINCE NEPTUNE IS SO **COOL.**
WOOZER
HAIRY OTTER
CHEPS

HE'S SO... DREAMY.
**NEXT TIME, ON SOLAR SISTERS...**
CLICK
NEWTFLAX
SEPT.

HOPE I DON'T RUIN ELMA'S SKETCHBOOK... NOT THAT SHE'LL NOTICE.

"MY DARLING PRINCE NEPTUNE. I DON'T THINK YOU'RE EVIL. ONLY... MISUNDERSTOOD."

"PRINCESS DANIELLE, YOU'RE SO TALENTED AND SMART. CLEARLY YOU SHOULD BE MY QUEEN INSTEAD."
"WELL, IF YOU INSIST..."

WOW, THAT ACTUALLY CAME OUT PRETTY GREAT. TAKE THAT, RHONDA.
BATTLEMAN

THOOP!

AHHH!!

MY BEAUTIFUL PRINCESS DANIELLE.

BOING
OW
ROLL ROLL

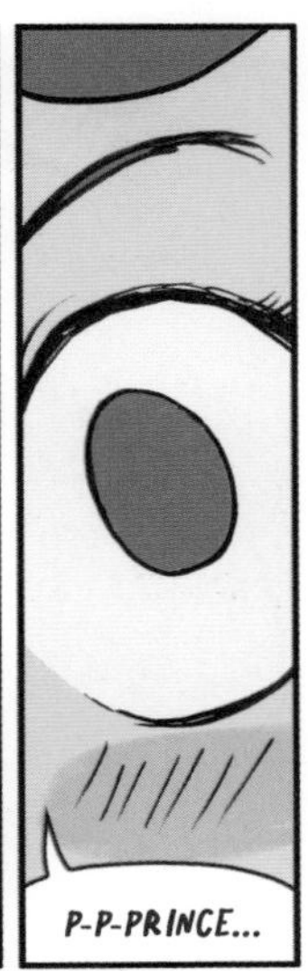
P-P-PRINCE...

NEPTUNE?
YOU'VE REALLY GOT TO TIDY YOUR **ROOM.**

ARE YOU **REAL?!**
POKE POKE
OW!

I APPEAR TO BE MISSING MY BODY, BUT AS FAR AS ANY OF US IS REAL...

I AM, INDEED, THE TRUE **PRINCE NEPTUNE.**

WOW. PRINCE NEPTUNE IS ALWAYS COOL, EVEN WHEN HE'S JUST A DISEMBODIED HEAD.

DANIELLE?
nok nok
BATTLEMAN

FOOP!
KEEP QUIET!

I HEARD A SCREAM!
OH, I JUST... STUBBED MY TOE ON SOMETHING.

OF COURSE YOU DID; YOUR ROOM IS A TOTAL MESS.
PLEASE, I BEG OF YOU, IF YOU LOVE ME AT ALL, CLEAN YOUR ROOM.
HAIRY OTTER

...MOM? WHAT DID AUNT ELMA DO? WHO WAS SHE?
I ONLY KNEW HER WHEN I WAS A LITTLE GIRL. SHE WAS AN ODD DUCK.
APPARENTLY FABULOUSLY WEALTHY, SO I GUESS I SHOULD HAVE BEEN FRIENDLIER.
SO YOU DON'T KNOW ANYTHING ABOUT HER?

I THINK SHE WAS INTO THE OCCULT. I WAS TERRIFIED OF HER, SO I NEVER GOT TO KNOW HER VERY WELL.
YOUR AUNT HAS HER DIARIES, YOU KNOW. MAYBE SHE'LL LET YOU BORROW THEM.

THAT'S UNLIKELY.
...WHY DOES SHE EVEN WANT THOSE OLD DIARIES?
MAYBE SHE WANTS TO KNOW IF ELMA BURIED GOLD IN THE BACKYARD.

NOW I WANT THE DIARIES!

HEY! THAT'S ENOUGH DISTRACTING ME, DANIELLE. CLEAN YOUR ROOM. THEN I NEED HELP WITH DINNER.

LAUREN IS MAKING A SALAD RIGHT NOW. WHAT A GREAT DAUGHTER SHE IS.
ALL RIGHT, I GET IT! I'LL CLEAN MY ROOM ALREADY!

GRRR
heh
heh
LAUREN'S ROOM IS ALREADY CLEAN.

A BEAUTIFUL PRINCESS SUCH AS YOURSELF SHOULDN'T HAVE TO DO SUCH MENIAL TASKS.

FWOOOO

FOLD!

UKE

WOW!
UKE CHORDS

MAGICAL POWERS ARE REALLY QUITE **USEFUL**, MY LOVELY PRINCESS DANIELLE.

I'M NOT ACTUALLY A PRINCESS.
A PRINCESS WITHOUT HER KINGDOM IS **STILL** A PRINCESS, DEAR DANIELLE.
BATTLEMAN

IT'S NOT LIKE SOMEONE TOOK AWAY MY KINGDOM. I NEVER **HAD** ONE. I'M JUST YOUR RUN-OF-THE-MILL, AVERAGE TWELVE-YEAR-OLD GIRL.

I'M SORRY, BUT I DON'T BELIEVE YOU.
BATTLEMAN

YOU SAW MY MOM, RIGHT? DO YOU THINK SHE'S THE QUEEN?
BATTLEMAN
MAYBE SHE'S NOT YOUR REAL MOM. MAYBE SHE KIDNAPPED YOU AS A BABY FROM THE REAL CELESTIAL QUEEN.

I'M SORRY, I BROUGHT YOU INTO A WORLD THAT IS PRETTY UNEXCITING AND UNMAGICAL.
pat
pat

I HAVE TO GO TO DINNER. YOU DON'T EAT, RIGHT?

YOU SUBSIST ON STARLIGHT AND... UM... HUMAN ENERGY?
PRINCESS DANIELLE, YOU ARE MOST SAGACIOUS AND WORLDLY.

I'M GOING TO NEED YOU TO HANG OUT HERE. NO OFFENSE, BUT YOU'D TOTALLY FREAK OUT MY PARENTS.
YOU CAN READ SOME BOOKS, WATCH TV...
WAVE

HNGHH
...
skritch
HELPME

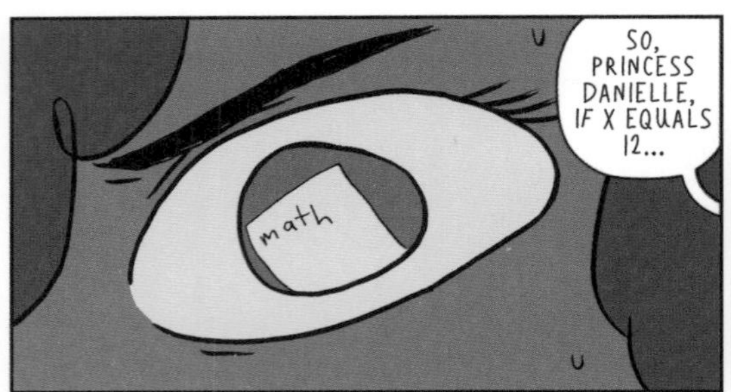
math
SO, PRINCESS DANIELLE, IF X EQUALS 12...

BUT HOW DO I FIND **Y?**

YOU KNOW THE ANSWER TO THIS, PRINCESS DANIELLE. ISOLATE THE Y VARIABLE.
CARRY THE ONE!
YEAH, YEAH.

OH, PRINCE NEPTUNE. IF ONLY **YOU** COULD BE MY MATH TEACHER.
I WOULD GIVE YOU AN **A.**

WELL... MAYBE A B+.

HEY, MAYBE I SHOULD TEST OUT MY MAGIC SKETCHBOOK. DRAW MY HOMEWORK FOR TOMORROW. JUST TO SEE IF IT'LL WORK.

FWOOO
BUT YOU WON'T **LEARN** THAT WAY.

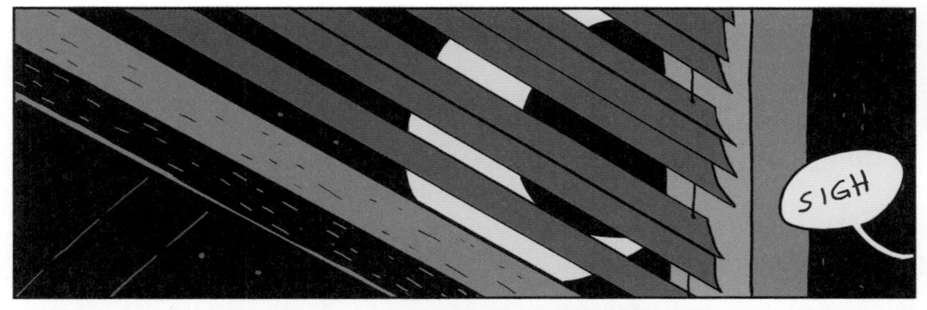
SIGH

WHAT AM I GOING TO **DO** WITH YOU?

YOU CAN'T GO OUT INTO THE WORLD.
YOU'RE A **BODILESS HEAD;** YOU'LL **SCARE** PEOPLE.

IF I COULD ACCOMPANY YOU ON YOUR JOURNEYS, PERHAPS IN A SATCHEL OF FINE SILK--

YOU MEAN MY BACKPACK? WON'T YOU BE BORED?

ANY TIME WITH PRINCESS DANIELLE,
WHOM I MAINTAIN IS STILL A PRINCESS AND JUST NEEDS TO GET HER KINGDOM BACK,
IS TRULY A GIFT.

AWW.

ALTHOUGH... THE STARLIGHT IS QUITE FAINT TONIGHT.

YEAH, THAT'S POLLUTION FOR YA. I READ THAT THE STARS USED TO BE REALLY BRIGHT BEFORE WE INVENTED CARS AND ELECTRICITY.

HUMANITY TRULY IS A **SCOURGE** UPON THE EARTH.
RIGHT? HUMANITY SUCKS.

WELL, I GUESS YOU COULD TAKE SOME OF MY ENERGY, IF IT'LL HELP ME SLEEP.
THANK YOU, PRINCESS DANIELLE.

GLOWW
JUST NOT **TOO** MUCH. I DON'T WANT TO **DIE.**

FWOOO

MELTON MIDDLE SCHOOL
HA HA HA!!

I'D RATHER DATE HIM THAN DATE YOU!
...

OKAY.

good one bro
BUMP

NICK! DANIELLE!
YOU'RE BEING DISRUPTIVE! ONE MORE PEEP AND IT'S DETENTION!
TURN
TURN

WAHHH

?
SLAM!

SOB!

WHAT IS A GOOD COMEBACK FOR THAT?!

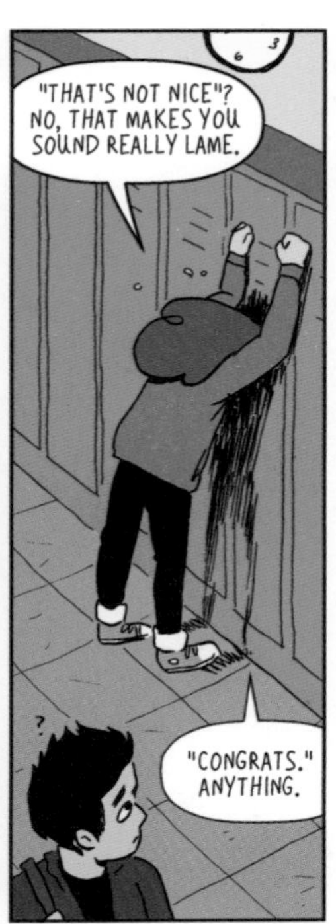
"THAT'S NOT NICE"? NO, THAT MAKES YOU SOUND REALLY LAME.
"CONGRATS." ANYTHING.

"I DON'T WANT TO DATE YOU, EITHER"? (OBVIOUSLY!)

OH, MAYBE– "I'D RATHER DATE KEVIN THAN DATE YOU, TOO!" NO...THAT'S TOO EMBARRASSING.
hm

PRINCESS DANIELLE!

WHO HAS HARMED YOU?!
WRFRINK!

STUPID NICK TOLD ME HE'D RATHER DATE KEVIN THAN ME.
NOT THAT I ASKED HIS OPINION ON THE SUBJECT.

HOW DARE THOSE INSIGNIFICANT ANTS SPEAK THUSLY TO THE PRINCESS OF THEIR REALM?

OH, NEPTUNE. NOW YOU KNOW THE TERRIBLE TRUTH ABOUT ME.
I'M...

UNPOPULAR.

SOME OF THE **GREATEST DESPOTS** IN **GANYMEDE** WERE UNPOPULAR.

IS THAT SUPPOSED TO MAKE ME FEEL BETTER?!

HUMANS ARE ATTRACTED TO WEAKNESS.
THEY LONG TO EXPLOIT IT. YOU MUST QUASH YOUR WEAKNESSES.

WELL, WHAT WAS I **SUPPOSED** TO SAY?
HOW ABOUT:

"YOU IMPERIL YOUR MEANINGLESS LIFE BY POKING AT THE HIDE OF A FAR MORE POWERFUL BEAST THAN YOU."

SO I'M A **BEAST** NOW? I THOUGHT I WAS A **PRINCESS.**

FAIR POINT.

IF ONLY I HAD SOMEONE TO BACK ME UP...

TO BE MY FRIEND, TO BE BY MY SIDE...

I WOULD BE THAT FOR YOU AND **MORE,** MY PRINCESS!
Float
IF YOU BUT **ASK,** I WILL ACCOMPANY YOU AND TEAR THE LIMBS FROM ANY HUMAN WHO CAUSES YOU DISTRESS.
Physical Education

YOU CAN'T JUST GO AROUND **MURDERING** PEOPLE!

AND ANYWAY, YOU'RE JUST A FLOATY HEAD!

NO. I THINK I'VE GOT A...
GLINT!
**PRETTY GENIUS IDEA.**

Fw
tackle!
teamwork!
GO WILD BEAR
interception!

NEPTUNE! **GEEZ!** YOU'RE GONNA BLOW MY COVER!
BACK INTO THE **SATCHEL,** I SUPPOSE?
tackle!
teamwork!
GO WILD BEAR

YOU ARE BEAUTIFUL

skritch!

...HER NAME IS **MADISON.**
I ♥ RODRIGO
I HATE CARA! why IDK...

MADISON... UMMM...

HM...

UHH...
nibble

NO...
you can do it!
Shut up Tiffany
Asbestos

MADISON SHOE?

FONTAINE
THAT'S **IT!**
Whelan

MADISON **FONTAINE!** HOW FANCY!

MADISON FONTAINE. SHE JUST MOVED HERE FROM... NEW YORK CITY.
SHE'S REALLY COOL, FUNNY, SMART, AND IS MY NEW BEST FRIEND.
ch. 4 questions 3-25
SHE THINKS I'M INTERESTING.
SHE ALWAYS HAS A SNAPPY REPLY AND IS ADVENTUROUS AND KNOWS BIG WORDS AND HOW TO DO HAIR AND MAKEUP REALLY WELL, AND SHE'LL MAKE ME PRETTY.
HOME WORK A+
SHE IS IN ALL MY CLASSES AND HAS MY LUNCH WAVE AND IS AWESOME.
NOTE

POOF
GAH!

IT'S **CROWDED** IN HERE, **YEESH!**

M-MADISON?

HEY, DANY!

I'M SO PSYCHED WE'RE IN ALL THE SAME CLASSES!
WHAT ARE THE CHANCES?
FLOAT
HYUCK!
YOU ARE BEAUTIFUL
THANKS MOM
Y-YEAH! ME TOO!
OH MY GOSH, DANY, ARE YOU CRYING?
NOT ANYMORE!
I JUST--
NICK MALONEY SAID HE'D RATHER DATE KEVIN THAN ME, LIKE...

OOH, WHEN'S THE **WEDDING?**
THIS IS WHY I NEED YOU AROUND! PERFECT COMEBACKS!

BACCPACC
I THOUGHT **MY** COMEBACK WAS BETTER.

**HOLY CANNOLI!** WHAT IS GOING ON?!

UM.

DANY, WHY DO YOU HAVE A **TALKING HEAD** IN YOUR BACKPACK?

THIS IS PRINCE NEPTUNE.

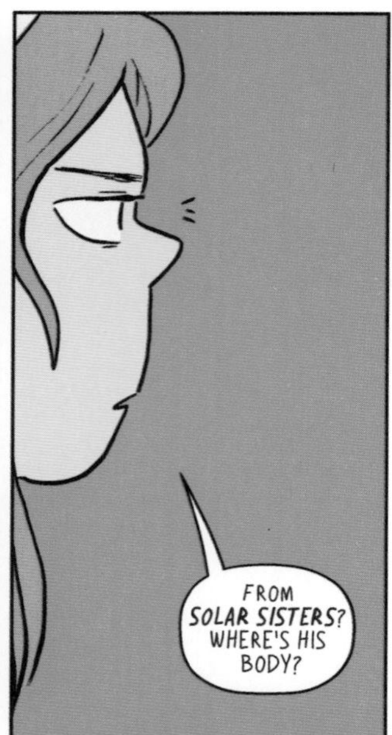
FROM **SOLAR SISTERS**? WHERE'S HIS BODY?

I DO NOT POSSESS ONE AT PRESENT.

WOW! A FLOATY HEAD!
FWISH FWISH

***EXCELLENT*** IDEA, PRINCESS DANIELLE. NOW YOU HAVE A MAIDSERVANT TO PROTECT YOU FROM ***RUFFIANS.***
FWOOOO
FREEDOM

I'M NOT SOME STUPID **MAIDSERVANT!**
I'M...
UM...
NEW STUDENT TRANSFER:
Madison L. Fontaine
YOU ARE BEAUTIFUL
thanks mom
...OH, DANY. LOOK AT YOU. I CAN'T LET YOU OUT THERE LOOKING LIKE YOU'RE SAD.

TA-DA!

BLOT

HAND ME MY KABUKI BRUSH.
I DON'T KNOW WHAT THAT IS.
CREEM

THANKS, DUDE.
FWOO

YOU ARE BEAUTIFUL
Thanks mom

THAT'S HOW WE DO IT IN THE BIG APPLE!
OKAY, I GOTTA GIVE THIS NOTE TO THE OFFICE.
I'LL MEET YOU IN CLASS!
note
...

COOL
GIRL
WOW

AREN'T YOU SUPPOSED TO BE IN **CLASS,** SLACKER?

I... I CAN'T FIND MY ***HOMEWORK!***
HISSTORY
B+

THEY'RE GONNA SEND A NOTE HOME TO MY PARENTS IF I DON'T HAVE IT.

BUT I REALLY DID IT!

IT'S IN HERE **SOMEWHERE...**

YOU NEED A BINDER.
I KNOW, I KNOW.

ACTUALLY, YOU NEED ABOUT **EIGHT** BINDERS AND A **LIFESTYLE GURU.**
ALGEBRA

I'M SUCH A HYPOCRITE.
IS IT THIS?
NO, IT'S A SCIENCE REPORT.

I LIVED A GOOD LIFE.

TOM'S SCIENCE REPORT.

SCIENCE
HIS HOMEWORK ASSIGNMENT FROM LAST NIGHT.

I LEFT IT AT HOME. **AGAIN.** MY PARENTS ARE GONNA KILL ME.
POOF

I FOUND IT!
?!
FROGS: SO MANY FROGS

THIS--
THIS IS
IT!

THANK YOU, DANIELLE! YOU SAVED MY LIFE!
NO PROB!

I'LL...

I'LL ORGANIZE THIS STUFF LATER.
KICK

Be true

CLASS, THIS IS **MADISON.** SHE JUST MOVED HERE FROM ***NEW YORK CITY.***
We the People...
—Thomas Edison
DOROTHEA DIX —
- insane asylum reform
Sit here!!

hiya, peeps
PLEASE DO WHAT YOU CAN TO HELP MADISON FEEL AT HOME.

MADDIE! YOU CAN SIT NEXT TO ME, IF YOU WANT.

I'M CARA. CARA MCCOY.

ALEESHA WILL MOVE. MY DAD IS FROM NYC, SO WE'LL--
...

AW YEAH, NEIGHBORS!
what

DON'T WORRY, CARA, THIS SEAT'S GOOD.

ELTON
IDDLE
CHOOL est. 1962

ha ha
zzzp!

WHERE TO NOW, GIRLS?
...

ACTUALLY, NEPTUNE, CAN YOU MEET US AT HOME?

...GLADLY. I NEED TIME TO RECOVER FROM THE SCREECHING OF HUMAN STUDENTS ALL DAY.
MY HEADACHE ENERVATES ME.

FWOOOO
humans...
UM...

IS IT COOL FOR HIM TO BE ON HIS OWN?
I'M KINDA BEHIND ON **SOLAR SISTERS**, BUT ISN'T PRINCE NEPTUNE, LIKE... **EVIL?**
HE'S JUST **MISUNDERSTOOD!**
WE SHOULD DO SOMETHING REALLY **FUN.**
YEAH? LIKE WHAT?
I DUNNO! I JUST DON'T FEEL LIKE GOING HOME YET.

ACTUALLY, I KINDA, UM... FORGET WHERE HOME **IS.**

AREN'T YOUR PARENTS... STILL IN NEW YORK?
F-FINISHING BUSINESS?

WELL, YEAH, **DUH.** I GUESS THEY'D STILL BE FINALIZING BUYING THE HOUSE.

AND OF COURSE YOU'RE STAYING AT **MY** PLACE IN THE MEANTIME.

OF COURSE. HAH. IF I DIDN'T HAVE MY HEAD SCREWED ON...
YOU'D BE LIKE PRINCE NEPTUNE!

HA HA HA HA

IS THERE A MALL AROUND HERE?

"IS THERE A MALL AROUND HERE?"
heh

IT'S THE **SUBURBS!** THE MALL IS OUR **LIFEBLOOD!** IT IS THE PULSING CENTER OF MELTON'S VERY **SOUL!**

I LOVE THE MALL!
ME TOO!

CHECK THIS OUT.

I GOT THIS COOL MAGICAL SKETCHBOOK FROM MY DEAD GREAT-AUNT!
um...

m-magic is real?!

IS THIS REAL?!
FLIP!

YEAH, IT IS. ISN'T THAT CRAZY?!
WHAT *ELSE* CAN YOU DO WITH THAT THING?

...MAGIC RINGS THAT ENABLE THEIR WEARERS TO *FLY*.

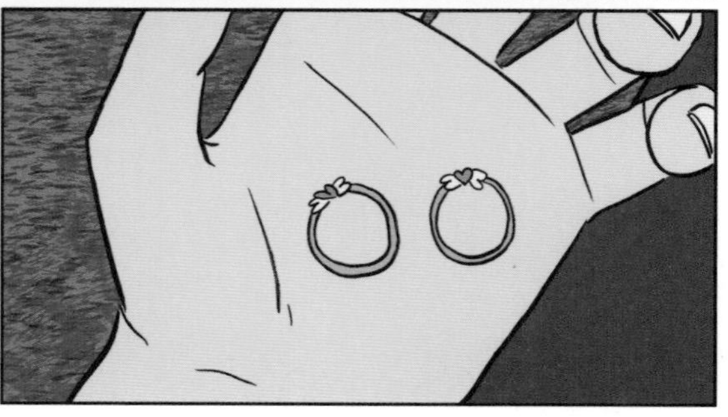

DANY!!
TRY THE RING ON, MADISON! THIS IS...

FWOOSH!

AWESOME!

WHEEEEEEE

OH WOW, IT'S CHILLY UP HERE.
DUH! THAT'S HOW THE *SKY* WORKS.

HEY GUYS, WHAT'S UP?
ha ha ha
QUACK

SURF'S UP!
FWOOSH!

MALL
THERE IT IS!

THE MALL!
MALL
WHAT A WONDERFUL PLACE TO BE.

LET'S LAND IN THAT LADY'S SHOPPING CART.
NO WAY! I DON'T WANT PEOPLE ASKING QUESTIONS. THEY'D TAKE MY SKETCHBOOK AWAY!
OUR FLYING RINGS HAVE **SOME** CLOAKING, BUT WE'RE NOT ***INVISIBLE...***

***DUMPSTERVILLE.*** JUST THE KIND OF ***GRAND ENTRANCE*** GIRLS WITH THE ***POWER OF FLIGHT*** DESERVE.
WE'VE GOT TO STAY INCONSPICUOUS!
NO DUMPING

10% OFF GOING OUT OF BUSINESS
ANOOYOO
SO!
WHAT DOES THE **COOL NEW ME** WEAR?
MEET THE NEW YOU
ANOOYOO
DIRECTORY
INFO
TRASH
RIGHT 'N' NARROW
TECHNOLOGY
She's back + looking for love
SLIMMER 2!
POOKIE
POOKIE

WEAR WHATEVER MAKES YOU HAPPY! EVEN IF IT'S...
CANDY from GRAMMA
Shoes for her

...T-SHIRTS THAT REACH YOUR KNEES...
GAMES
VIDEO
OFTEN 35
YOU ARE SO CLOSE TO style
Stoar
Maybe get a Phone
iFur

WHAT'S THE MATTER WITH AQUATIC LASER SCOTT? HE'S GOT A TRAGIC PAST!

NOTHING, NOTHING! YOU JUST DON'T HAVE TO HIDE YOUR BODY, YOU KNOW?

I HAVE NO IDEA WHAT YOU'RE TALKING ABOUT.
SO CLOSE + YET
Sofa
NOTHI GOOD™
CHELTZER

PEARL JORM

INTERNET

CUTIE

eh?

It's the NEW ME!

TRY SOMETHING THAT'S YOUR STYLE, THAT REFLECTS WHO YOU ARE...

BUT I DON'T WANT TO BE ME!

I JUST WANNA BE COOOOL

SAID NO COOL PERSON EVER.
WELL IT'S A PARADOX OR SOMETHING!

HOW CAN YOU BE COOL WHEN **TRYING** TO BE COOL MAKES YOU **NOT** COOL?
BECAUSE PEOPLE CAN SMELL YOUR DESPERATION.
FROOZE

JUST, LIKE, **EXIST.** EXIST WHILE NOT CARING WHAT OTHER PEOPLE THINK.
mhm...
SKritch!
29.95 is a pretty good price!

Boyfriend
SKINNY

Boyfriend
SKINNY

SKINNY

Am I COOL yet?!
OH, FOR SURE.

BOOK WHO'S TALKING!
J.D. BOBB
New Hit series
This rookie has earned her OVERTIME
ANACHRONISM
new notable BOOKS
...OF COURSE I LOVE MORPHIMALS! I'VE READ LIKE THIRTY OF THE BOOKS SO FAR!
YA
WAVERLEY PREP
#34 CAME OUT LAST WEEK.
MORPHIMALS

I KNOW THEY'RE FOR, LIKE, FOURTH GRADERS, BUT I GOTTA KNOW IF THEY DEFEAT THE ALIENS.
I'VE INVESTED SO MUCH TIME AT THIS POINT.
MORPHIMALS

OH, DANY, YOU'D **LOVE** THIS BOOK.
OPHELIA'S TEARS

AND THIS ONE.
THWUMP!
THE HUMAN CHRONICLES
VOL 1
"A WORK OF UNFETTERED GENIUS!"
AND THIS ONE. JUST TRUST ME, YOU WON'T BE ABLE TO PUT IT DOWN.

HOW ARE WE GONNA CARRY ALL THESE BOOKS?!
MAGIC?
SMART THINGS

REWARDS
IT'S TASTY, TOO
OUI
all's smell that ends smell!
FANCY
you so fancy

AAHH! NO! THAT ONE SMELLS LIKE BUTTS!
SPRITZ!
BABY
ACK! TOO MUCH!

OUT!
ha ha cough ha
KOFF KOFF
TEST OU
SCENTS

CORPORATE LOGOS ARE COUNTER-CULTURE!
COOL SUBJECT
GOT COUCH?
koff koff
ha ha
GET OUTTA CHAIR

SOLAR SISTERS

I... NEED THIS...

...AND THIS, AND THIS...

OH MY GOD, IS THIS WHAT BEING RICH IS LIKE?
IS THIS WHAT I'VE BEEN MISSING OUT ON MY WHOLE LIFE?
COOLDAD
PLUSHEE'S!

MMM
MEGA BUN

WE SHOULD GO HOME SOON.
BOO.
BUN
MEGA

UM...
YOUR PARENTS DEFINITELY KNOW I'M COMING OVER?

OH YEAH. W-WE TOLD THEM A WHILE AGO.

I MIGHT HAVE TO JOG THEIR MEMORIES, THOUGH.
ISN'T IT KINDA...

...IRRESPONSIBLE FOR MY PARENTS TO SEND ME OFF BY MYSELF LIKE THIS?
BILL DING'S BUILDING BUILDERS
SEERS
PSYCHIC SUPPLIES
COOL

...I'M SURE THEY JUST **TRUST** YOU, IS ALL.
Melton 5
Bridgeford 9
Puppytown 16
Trombull Mall
THIS EXIT
mocy
Lord & Vader
Mag

...

I GUESS SO.

I JUST FEEL LIKE I'M **HOMELESS** OR SOMETHING.

UM, MOM?

MY FRIEND MADISON...

HER PARENTS ARE OUT OF TOWN AND I TOLD HER SHE COULD STAY WITH US.
IS THAT OKAY?

AS LONG AS YOUR **PARENTS** ARE OKAY WITH IT.
HOME

YEAH, THEY DON'T REALLY CARE.
THANKS, MRS. RADLEY!
WELL, HOLD YOUR THANKS UNTIL YOU GET A LOOK AT DANIELLE'S BEDROOM. IT'S LIKE A WAR ZONE IN THERE.

**I CLEANED IT!!!!**

WHAT'S THIS? DANIELLE HAS A ***FRIEND?***
THAT'S MY BIG SISTER, LAUREN.

I DON'T KNOW WHY YOU SOUND SO SHOCKED THAT I HAVE A ***FRIEND.***

HOW MUCH IS SHE PAYING YOU?

I'M PAYING HER IN FRIENDSHIP POINTS.
ha ha ha
EVERY 100 POINTS I GET A FREE ICE CREAM SUNDAE!

MOM, WAS **I** THAT DORKY WHEN I WAS IN SEVENTH GRADE, OR IS DANIELLE JUST **SPECIAL**?
YOU'RE BOTH SPECIAL.

WOULD YOU LIKE **HELP** WITH ANYTHING, MRS. RADLEY?
no no no no noooo

NO, NO, YOU GIRLS GO PLAY.
FFWOOOSHH
THIS WAY!

DANY
Neptune?

DEAREST PRINCESS DANIELLE!
SOLAR SISTERS

...AND MADISON. **YOU'RE** STILL HANGING AROUND.
PLOP!
SOLAR

...

WHERE ELSE WOULD SHE BE?

MAYBE WITH MY PARENTS.

S-SORRY...

I'VE BEEN THINKING ABOUT THAT MARVELOUS **SKETCHBOOK** OF YOURS, DANIELLE.

NOT THAT I **MIND** MY CURRENT STATE, BUT PERHAPS I COULD ACCOMPANY YOU TO SCHOOL IN A LESS...

...**UNCOUTH...** MANNER IF I WERE TO POSSESS A BODY OF MY **OWN.**

WHAT WOULD ***YOU*** DO WITH A BODY?

WOULD YOU, PERHAPS, HARNESS HUMAN ENERGY AND TRY TO DESTROY THE PLANET?
ZAP!
HAHAHA
FWIP

I DID THAT ***ONE TIME.*** AND I APOLOGIZED.
I LEARNED A LESSON ABOUT THE NATURAL BEAUTY OF PLANET EARTH.

HE ***DID*** APOLOGIZE! SEASON 3.
OH, I'M STILL IN SEASON 2.

I ***GUESS*** I CAN TRY DRAWING YOU A BODY.
FLOP

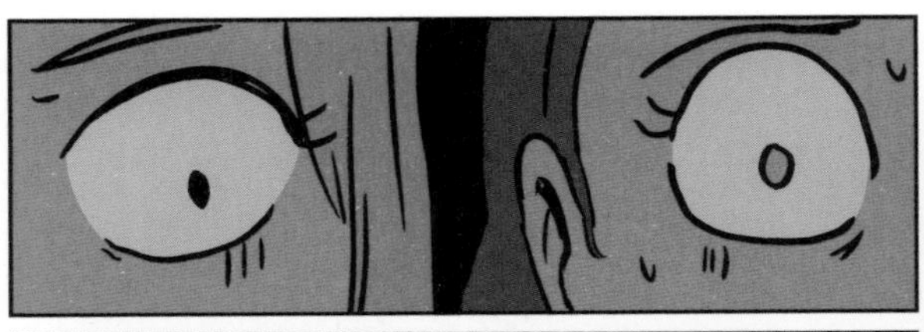

DID I DO IT WRONG? IT'S ALL...COLD.
POKE!

TWITCH!

AHHHHHHH
LURCH

PRINCESS DANIELLE, I AM MERELY MANIPULATING-- THIS VESSEL'S EXTREMITIES--

OF WHICH, THERE ARE SO MANY--
LURCH

WAVE

AHHHHHH

I CAN BLEND IN SEAMLESSLY AT SCHOOL LIKE THI--

WOOSH

NEPTUNE!
GRAB
THUMPLE!

UKE CHORDS
z-zombie....
ARE YOU OKAY?

MY TELEKINETIC ABILITIES... ARE NOT BOUNDLESS. IF I COULD HARVEST SOME--

NO HARVESTING!
sigh

YEAH, NO HARVESTING.

OKAY, WE NEED TO GET RID OF THIS BODY. OTHERWISE I'M GOING TO FIND A NICE PARK BENCH TO SLEEP ON TONIGHT.
I DON'T WANT TO TOUCH IT.
MUCH OF MY ENERGY HAS ALREADY BEEN EXPENDED. UNLESS THERE IS A HUMAN ENERGY SOURCE YOU CAN SPARE.
SPOOKY

FWOO
LET'S NEVER EVER TALK ABOUT THIS AGAIN, OKAY?
I'LL NEVER BE OKAY.

BRUSH

SHE DOESN'T KNOW.
FSHHHH

I HAVE TO TELL HER, BUT... I JUST DIDN'T WANT TO MAKE HER SAD.
MADISON MUST BE A FOOL NOT TO REALIZE HER PROVENANCE IS YOUR MAGICAL SKETCHBOOK.

SHE EMERGED FROM ITS PAGES, JUST AS I DID.
Solar Sisters
ALTHOUGH IN MY CASE, I BELIEVE I WAS SIMPLY SPIRITED TO THIS DIMENSION, SINCE I CLEARLY EXISTED IN SOME CAPACITY PRIOR TO MY ARRIVAL.

SHE'S NOT A FOOL! SHE JUST ASSUMES SHE'S...

SHE'S JUST, LIKE, MAGICAL OR WHATEVER.
"REAL"?
SHE IS REAL!
...AND HOMELESS.

OH, GOD, WHAT HAVE I DONE?
FWOMP

YOU CREATED A GIRL. ANYONE ELSE WOULD BE IMPRESSED WITH THAT ACCOMPLISHMENT.

BUT YOU, PRINCESS DANIELLE, ARE SUCH A BASTION OF MODESTY--
oh pshaw

BUT HOW DO I TELL HER SHE DOESN'T HAVE A FAMILY?

I DON'T WANT TO MAKE HER SAD.

FAMILY. **HAH!** FAMILY IS OVERRATED.

**MY** LOVING PARENTS SOLD ME TO THE **DRAGON LORD** AS A SMALL BOY, IN RETURN FOR THEIR KINGDOM.

BUT THEY WERE BETRAYED BY THE DRAGON LORD AND MURDERED.
**SPOILERS!**

THAT WAS **SO** SAD!
ALSO, MADISON, I HAVE THE **SOLAR SISTERS** COMICS HERE, IF YOU WANT TO GET AHEAD OF THE SHOW.

I PROTEST THAT THOSE BOOKS PROVIDE A RATHER ONE-SIDED PORTRAYAL OF ME.

IT'S OKAY, PRINCE NEPTUNE. I WAS ALWAYS A FAN.
I THOUGHT YOU GOT A BAD RAP.

NO ONE UNDERSTANDS YOUR DARKNESS.

JUST LIKE DANIELLE.
MY HEART IS DARK AND FULL OF PAIN.

STOP
z z z

EXIT
SCHOOL BUS IT'S NE
WAVE
yawn

WOW, DANIELLE! YOU LOOK SO... COOL!

YEAH, MADISON AND I WENT TO THE MALL YESTERDAY.
I TAKE ANY AND ALL CREDIT FOR DANY LOOKING FASHIONABLE.

I WANT A MAKEOVER.

YOU CAN'T YELL AT ME IF WE HIT A BUMP AND I COMPLETELY RUIN YOUR FACE.
I CAN GET A MAKEOVER LATER.

GOOD JOB KIDS

who's the babe?
MARINES

GROSS, DANIEL! THAT'S WAY TOO MUCH SKIN.
That's my niece! She's six months old
aw

"GROSS"
Gross, Daniel
Gross Daniel
"GROSS"
"DANIEL"
GROSS DANIEL
GROSS, DANIEL
Gross Daniel
GROSS, DANIEL
CENSORED
"DANIEL"
CENSORED
GROSS
DANIEL
WHY ARE YOU SO INSECURE...
SLAM!
BOO HOO

THAT YOU FEEL THE NEED TO TARGET MY FRIEND...
MY HERO

...IN ORDER TO FEEL BETTER ABOUT YOURSELF?

AHH! YOU'RE CRAZY!

YOU WANT TO SEE CRAZY? I'LL SHOW YOU CRAZY.

YOU SAY ONE WORD TO DANY THAT ISN'T FLOWERS AND SUNSHINE,
AND YOU'LL SEE JUST HOW CRAZY I CAN BE.

heh
fight?
hn?
KNOCK

GO ON, RUN OFF, YOU ANNOYING MANBABY.

owned by a CHICK!
man baby!
haha
haha
STOMP
STOMP

OH, MADISON, YOU **SAVED** ME!
THAT'S WHAT FRIENDS ARE FOR!

GOOF

hee hee
GIRLS, GO TO **SLEEP!**

VFA
THEATERS
THE WOOGLIES
PRIMAL RELATIONS
CINEMA
YOU'VE SERIOUSLY NEVER SNUCK INTO A RATED-R MOVIE BEFORE?
TEACH ME!
OKAY, FOLLOW MY LEAD.
KINGTON
BREAKER of CODES
FARTS IN ATLANTIS

TWO TICKETS FOR *THE WOOGLIES,* PLEASE!
WOOGLIES 2D
DIGITAL
RATED
G
7:30PM
AUD 3
Ticket Stub
PRIMAL R 7:15
NOT SUITABLE FOR MINORS
RATED
R
GO AWAY YOU BABIES
sneak
This has really good reviews actually
"OOH"
"MMM"
"OUI MONSIEUR"
I can't unshee thish
PRIMAL R 9:30
Shoulda seen Wooglies
Yikes

READ AN apple every Day
SODA life

THIS BOOK IS POPULAR! DO YOU LIKE IT?
THE Heart WANTS
Dude

**THE HEART WANTS**?

THIS IS MY *FAVE*. I TOTALLY MADE ALEESHA READ IT, TOO.
yeah

...WHEN BEN TELLS CHRISTINE HE H-HAD THE LOCKET THE WHOLE TIME...

**NOOOO,** YOU'RE GONNA RUIN MY MASCARA!

**I** THOUGHT HE WAS A LITTLE CREEPY AND POSSESSIVE.
I WOULDN'T WANT SOME GUY TO *FOLLOW* ME AROUND FOR, WHAT, **TWENTY YEARS?**
ORANG JUICE
5% healthy
ingredients: corn, orang Pebbles™ liquid

I WOULD!
FWIP!
tee hee
Snorf

**IF** HE'S HOT.

SAYS THE GIRL WHOSE **DREAM BOYFRIEND** IS AN EVIL PRINCE.
I CAN HEAL HIS HEART WITH MY **LOVE.**
JUICE

I WISH WE HAD COOL BOYS LIKE **BEN** AT THIS SCHOOL!
YEAH...
Sigh
THE Heart WANTS

I THINK EDWARD YANG FROM MARCHING BAND IS PRETTY CUTE.
ew
ALEESHA
POKE POKE
JUICE

THERE IS **LITERALLY** NO CUTE BOY IN OUR GRADE.
yeah
YOU ARE WHAT YOU EAT
Be an Apple Fritter

THOSE **EIGHTH GRADERS,** THOUGH...

LITE
CHEPS

WHAT A DIFFERENCE A **YEAR** MAKES.
yeah

SUNDRIES • NEWS • CA
EBT
mhm
blah
blah
feelings
CHEPS
$500
WINNE

what am I doing
CHEP
real grease flavor!
heh heh
CAR WAS

AVERT YOUR GAZE
Nutrition Facts
Calories: 180 per serving
Servings: 3.5
Ingredients: salt, sodium, potato-like substance, maltodextrin, flavor crystals (chlorine), sawdust, salt

rummage
CHEPS

Skinny Girl

THAT'S CONVENIEN
BEER • CANDY • NEWS • CHILDCARE
311
LOTTO
Because you hate having money
$5000
WHAT IS THAT STUFF?

VENIEN
• CANDY • NEWS • EGG SALAD
LOTTO
$5000
DON'T YOU THINK IF I WERE...
SHEPS

...SKINNIER...

I'D BE MORE POPULAR?

I THINK YOU LOOK BEAUTIFUL AS YOU ARE, PRINCESS DANIELLE.
AWW, THANK YOU. BUT EARTHLINGS ARE VERY JUDGMENTAL.
...

DO **NOT** MESS WITH YOUR BODY WITH **MAGIC! C'MON!**
YOU DON'T KNOW-- MAGIC COULD BE EVIL! IT COULD HURT YOU!
s-sorry

BUT...
IF YOU WANT TO LOSE WEIGHT, DO IT THE--

--DO IT THE RIGHT WAY! GIVE ME THOSE **CHIPS!**
CHEPS
don't fight
there's plenty of me

BUT WHY CAN'T I JUST DRINK **SKINNY POTION**?!

!
YOINK!

FWOOSHH

BOOP

KRRCH!

I CAN ALWAYS MAKE MORE SKINNY POTION.

DON'T MESS AROUND WITH YOUR **HEALTH!** YOU-- YOU COULD **DIE!**

OKAY, TO PUT IT IN YOUR TERMS-- DON'T YOU REMEMBER THAT EPISODE OF **WHAT'S IN THE DARK?!**
THE ONE WHERE THE GIRL TURNED INTO A PORCELAIN DOLL AND HER LIMBS ALL CRACKED OFF?
HOLY NAME CHURCH
DOES SATAN GIVE YOU FREE DONUTS?

C'MON, I'M **CLEARLY** TALKING ABOUT THE ONE WHERE THE GIRL DRINKS FREAKIN' **SKINNY POTION** AND GETS TINY AND HER MOM STEPS ON HER.
**FINE!**

LOOK, WHY DON'T YOU AND I JUST GO JOGGING? YOU COULD SET THE PACE; IT WOULD BE REALLY CHILL.
I... I DON'T WANT THE **NEIGHBORS** TO SEE ME...

WELL, **THAT'S** CONVENIENT.
**WHATEVER!** I'M EXERCISING RIGHT NOW, **MOM.**

35
WELCOME

NEPTUNE?

DO YOU MISS YOUR FAMILY? DO YOU WISH PRINCE SATURN WERE HERE WITH YOU?

I HAVE MADE PEACE WITH MY BROTHER'S DEATH.

PARTLY BECAUSE I EXACTED SUCH TOTAL REVENGE AGAINST LORD DRAGON.

DO YOU MISS **YOUR** FAMILY, MADISON?

NEPTUNE!

I...

MADISON...

I MUST BE A TERRIBLE DAUGHTER.

YOU'RE NOT! MADISON, THERE'S SOMETHING--

WHY ELSE WOULD THEY NOT, LIKE, CALL ME? OR EMAIL ME? THEY MUST HATE ME.

IF ONLY I KNEW WHAT I DID WRONG.
BUT IT'S LIKE SOMEONE ERASED MY MEMORY OF THEM.
IS THAT WEIRD?

YOU'RE NOT A TERRIBLE DAUGHTER! YOU'RE **AMAZING!**
YOU'RE— YOU'RE JUST **SPECIAL.**
SO SPECIAL THAT YOU...
JUST...
DON'T HAVE PARENTS.

I WAS IN A CAR CRASH AND, LIKE...

...GOT AMNESIA AND YOU WEREN'T SUPPOSED TO SPRING EVERYTHING ON ME AT ONCE, SO--

FOOLISH GIRL. YOU SIMPLY CAME FROM PRINCESS DANIELLE'S ENCHANTED SKETCHBOOK.
HA, HA.
what

WOULD I LIE TO YOU?

ARE YOU JOKING? YOU'RE A BAD GUY! OF COURSE YOU'D LIE TO ME! WHY SHOULD I BELIEVE YOU?

RIGHT, DANY?

...

THIS IS **MESSED UP.** I'M GONNA...

I'M GONNA FIND MY PARENTS. THERE'S A **RATIONAL EXPLANATION** FOR ALL THIS.
WE-- WE HAD A FIGHT. A WEIRDLY UNMEMORABLE FIGHT. THEY SENT ME AWAY TO CONNECTICUT.

THE ***LAME*** PART OF CONNECTICUT. NO ONE HERE EVEN HAS A BOAT.
sorry

GRAB!
**MAGIC PHONE!** CALL MY **PARENTS!**

NO MATCH FOUND FOR "PARENTS." DID YOU MEAN "KAREN"?

...

IT'S... IT'S **TRUE,** MADISON. YOU CAME FROM THE **SKETCHBOOK.**

NO, I DIDN'T! THAT WOULD MAKE ME LIKE, **A WEEK OLD!**

I WAS...LONELY, AND I WANTED A FRIEND. NO ONE IN CLASS WOULD TALK TO ME.

SO I'M... I'M NOT A...
...REAL PERSON?

I'M JUST YOUR MAGICAL WINGMAN?

YOU **ARE** REAL! LOOK AT YOU!
YOU'RE **FLESH AND BLOOD**— YOU HAVE **FREE WILL**--
FLIP

FLIP

NOTE
HOME WORK A+

JUST BECAUSE I BROUGHT YOU TO LIFE WITH MAGIC DOESN'T MEAN, LIKE-- IT DOESN'T MEAN ANYTHING.
RIP

IT DOESN'T MEAN I'M HOMELESS? AN ORPHAN?

J-JUST THINK-- WE CAN DESIGN YOU THE **PERFECT PARENTS!**
...I WISH **I** COULD DESIGN THE PERFECT PARENTS FOR **ME.**

MADISON?

I DON'T **WANT** TO DESIGN MY OWN PARENTS.
I WANT **REAL** PARENTS.

NOT FAKE, CREEPY **SKETCHBOOK-PEOPLE.**

I—I DON'T KNOW WHAT TO DO!

MAYBE YOU SHOULD DRAW A TIME MACHINE, GO BACK IN TIME, AND UNDRAW ME.

DON'T EVEN JOKE ABOUT THAT! THAT WOULD BE **MURDER!**

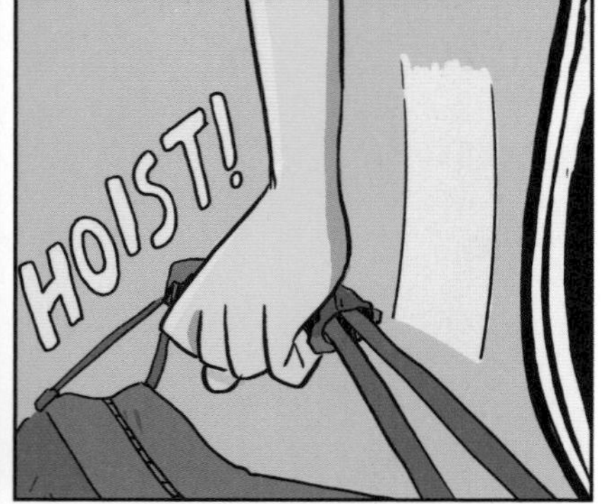
HOIST!

IT'S NOT MURDER IF IT'S JUST YOUR **IMAGINARY FRIEND.**

SHE DIDN'T TAKE **THAT** WELL, **DID** SHE?

sniff

COME BACK INSIDE, MADISON.

WE CAN FIGURE SOMETHING OUT. YOU-- YOU DON'T HAVE TO BE MY FRIEND ANYMORE IF YOU DON'T WANT TO.
BUT AT LEAST LET ME HELP YOU--

I DON'T HAVE TO BE YOUR FRIEND? WOULDN'T THAT BE GOING AGAINST MY PROGRAMMING?

NOT GREAT BOB
RIP

WHAT DO I DOOOOOOOOOO?

VOLUME
SAD DEATH
Greatest Hits
I'm so alone
S?d De?th
3:53

I QUITE LIKED THE TIME MACHINE IDEA. UNDRAW THAT MOPEY MAIDSERVANT AND WE CAN GET BIGGER PLANS UNDER WAY.
THAT'S NOT *FUNNY*.

STOP

MELTON MIDDLE SCHOOL
bye

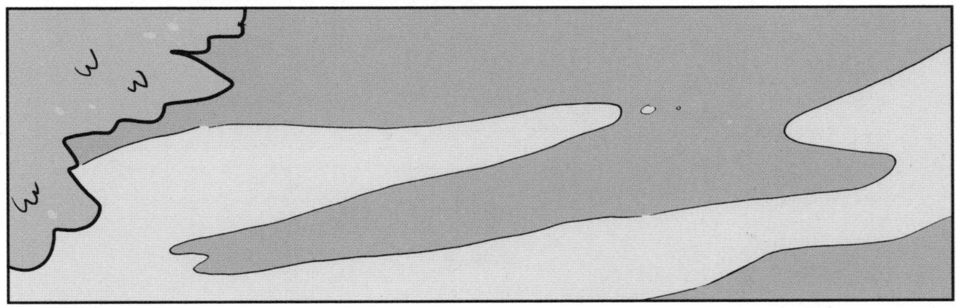

MADISON! DANY!

TURN
Don't make me go back...
I'M HAVING A PARTY ON SATURDAY NIGHT. INVITE WHOEVER. MY PARENTS ARE GONE ALL WEEKEND.
WON'T THEY GET MAD AT YOU?
NOT IF THEY DON'T FIND OUT.
Cara's Stuff
I'M IN!
THAT'S THE SAME DAY AS MY LITTLE COUSIN'S BIRTHDAY PARTY. I DON'T THINK I CAN GO.
OH, THAT'S FINE. NEXT TIME, DANY.
Cara's Stuff

I DON'T KNOW WHAT YOUR PARTIES ARE LIKE IN THE **BIG APPLE**, BUT YOU ARE GOING TO HAVE **SO MUCH FUN.**
BRING A SWIMSUIT; I'VE GOT A **POOL!**

huh
OKAY, BUT **PLEASE** TELL ME YOU'RE NOT INVITING KEN. I KNOW HE'S A FOOTBALL PLAYER, BUT I THINK HE'S BEEN HIT IN THE **HEAD** TOO MANY TIMES--
**OH MY GOD,** MADDIE! YOU'RE **TERRIBLE!**

KEN IS...

ha ha ha
uh
guys?

Oh my god, that was so LAME, I hope no one noticed me
...never mind...

GO WILD
MELTON CONNECTICUT
MIDDLE SCHOOL
GYM

HAPPY BIRTHDAY
Dr. gargle

SLURP

SMACK!

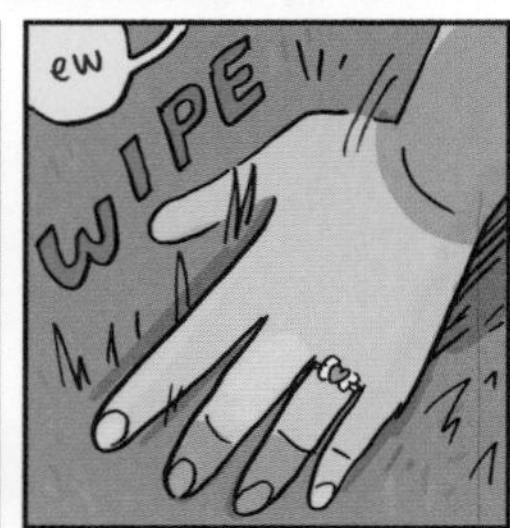
ew
WIPE

HAPPY BIRTHDAY
SIGH

...A MAGIC RING THAT WARDS OFF ALL MOSQUITOS AND BUGS AND UNWANTED PESTS.

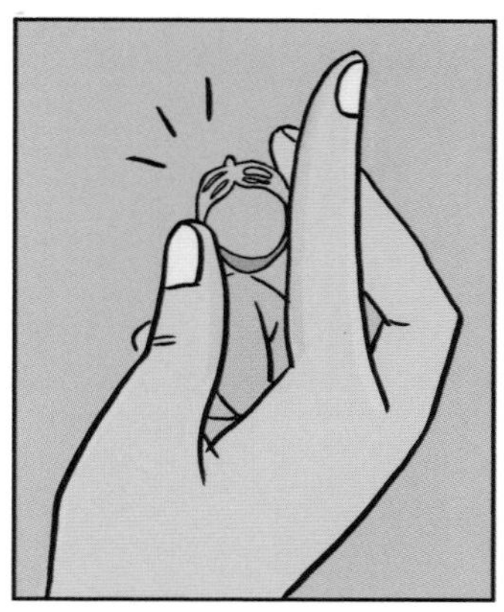

A TONKO TRUCK! WHAT DO YOU SAY TO AUNT TRACY?
I DON'T LIKE IT!

THAT'S **IT,** CHARLIE.

YOU KNOW WHAT?
YOU'RE NOT GETTING ANY BIRTHDAY CAKE.

NOOOOO!!!!

...

HRGH

EAAGH!!
Happy Birthday Charlie
SPLATT
pant
pant
WAHHHHH
HAPPY BIRTHDAY
...
WAAAAAHHHH

FOR GOD'S SAKE, DAVE...

HE DID THIS TO **HIMSELF.** THAT **SPOILED-ROTTEN ATTITUDE**--
WAAAA AH

YOU'RE TURNING INTO **DAD** MORE AND MORE EVERY **DAY.**

STOMP
STOMP
STOMP
STOMP

SLIDE
THE **CAKE!!** WHAT HAPPENED?
SPORX
WAAAAAAAAAAAHHHHHHHHHHH

WAAAAAAAAAAAAHHHHHH

WHAT'S WRONG WITH THE TRUCK I **GOT** YOU, HONEY?
I...
I LIKE **TRAINS**...

I'LL RETURN IT AND GET YOU A TRAIN. OKAY?
I'LL TAKE YOU TO THE TOY STORE... AND YOU CAN PICK OUT **ANY** TRAIN.

WIPE

DADDY IS JUST HAVING A "PSYCHOTIC BREAK." DO YOU KNOW WHAT A PSYCHOTIC BREAK IS?
sigh
TRACY, CUT IT OUT.
N-NO...

app y
irthd ay
harlie

blah blah sick of this
SIGH

I'M GONNA GO FOR A WALK. TELL MOM IT'S GETTING TOO CRAZY FOR ME IF SHE ASKS.
Promise me you'll euthanize me if I ever get like that, Linda
FINE.
**UGH,** I CAN'T BELIEVE HE RUINED THE **CAKE.**
I **ONLY** CAME HERE FOR THE CAKE.

awkward...
SLAM
SLAM
SLAM
SLAM
CONNECTICUT

HAPPY BIRTHD

INSTAGRAHAM
@realcaramccoy: swimsuit edition lmao
madmaam, oboelife3, and 200 others liked this!
@footballken wow lol

SPORTS

I'M AIMING FOR **CARA,** JUST FYI.
HAHAHA!
yeah
AWWW YEAH!

BIRTHDAY

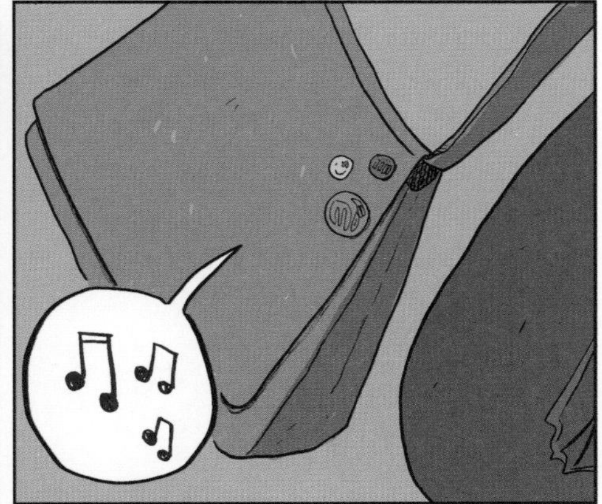

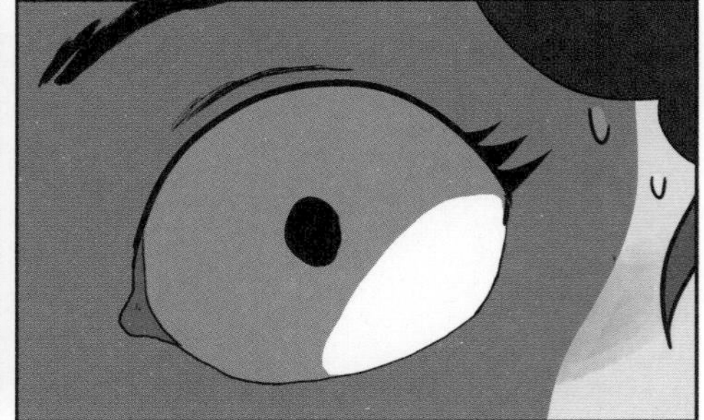

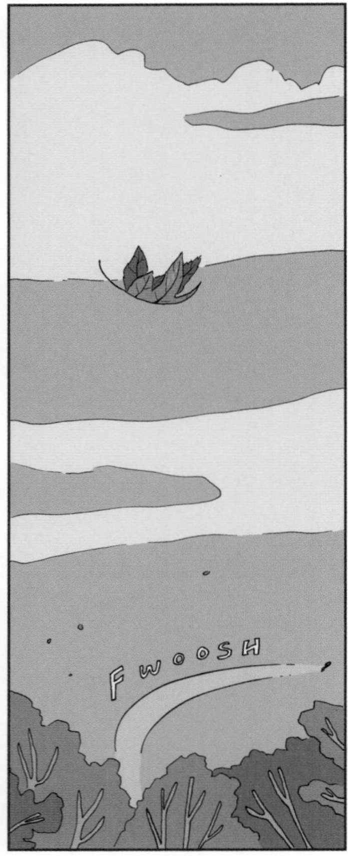
FWOOSH

FWOOSH!

MOM?
THE PARTY IS OVER.
...YEAH, DAVE, I GET IT, WE'RE ALL NEVER INVITED TO YOUR HOUSE AGAIN. EXCUSE ME WHILE I ROUND UP MY CHILDREN.

SORRY, HONEY.
WHERE ARE YOU?
I'M A FEW BLOCKS AWAY. I WANTED TO GET AWAY FROM...
I COMPLETELY UNDERSTAND.

YOUR BROTHER IS REALLY A PIECE OF WORK.

IS UNCLE DAVE REALLY HAVING A PSYCHOTIC BREAK?
HE'S HAVING A LOT OF TROUBLE AT THE LAB. HE'S ALSO A PIECE OF...

WORK. A PIECE OF WORK.

MAGELLAN
DID A THING

HE IS SUCH AN **IDIOT!**

EW, I KNOW! BUT HE HAS SUCH BEAUTIFUL EYES...
A BEAUTIFUL FACE WITH NOTHING GOING ON BEHIND IT. **TRAGIC.**

SO I'M GUESSING THE PARTY WAS FUN?

OH MAN, DANY, YOU MISSED ONE FOR THE AGES.
I'M GROUNDED FOR LIFE, BUT IT WAS SO WORTH IT.

I'M JEALOUS. MY COUSIN'S PARTY WAS PRETTY LAME, ALTHOUGH AT ONE POINT MY UNCLE THREW A CAKE ON THE GROUND--
ha
ha
OH MY GOD, REMEMBER WHEN KATIE FELL INTO THE POOL?

"ERUFFF!!"
ha
ha ha ha

HA HA
HA
heh

ha
IT KINDA SUCKS THAT HER PHONE BROKE, THOUGH.
ha ha
ha
ha
ha

She so broke up with Mosh Ha ha definitely
heh
ROCK LEGEND
CAFE
DANBURY

...

I'M KINDA SAD I MISSED THE PARTY.

YOU WOULD HAVE HAD FUN.
VOTE

PEP RALLY
soonish
**AND** YOU COULD HAVE MADE FRIENDS WITH SOME OF OUR CLASSMATES...
PUSH

AW MAN, I'M FAILING MY **MISSION,** AREN'T I?

"MISSION"?

I'M HERE TO HELP YOU MAKE FRIENDS, RIGHT?
AREN'T **WE** FRIENDS?
STAY IN SCHOOL KIDZ

OF COURSE WE ARE.

WELL THEN, MISSION COMPLETE. RESUME CIVILIAN DUTIES.

LOOK, MADISON, I DIDN'T HAVE SOME GRAND PLAN WHEN I...
WHEN I DREW YOU.

I JUST WANTED SOMEONE IN MY CLASS WHO ACTUALLY, LIKE, CARED ABOUT ME.
WELL, WHAT ABOUT WHAT I WANT.

I...

I HAVE TO GET TO MY LOCKER. LATER.

SHE TOTALLY HATES ME.

BUT YOU'RE SO MUCH BETTER THAN HER! YOU SHOULD BE THE ONE ALL THE OTHER GIRLS ASPIRE TO BEFRIEND.

HEH HEH. TELL ME MORE, PRINCE NEPTUNE.

WELL, FOR STARTERS, YOU'RE THE MOST BEAUTIFUL GIRL I'VE EVER LAID EYES UPON!
HAIR AS BROWN AS... WINTER LEAVES...
EYES... FILLED WITH WISDOM AND COURAGE...
AND SUCH ARTISTIC TALENT!
WHAT ELSE?!

ERM... YOUR...VIGOROUS ENTHUSIASM—
yay

TEACHERS ONLY
NUGGETS ARE BACK!
ha ha ha
Ha
Ha
Ha
NUGGETS
DANIELLE! HI!
OH, HI, TOM.
ROCK LEGEND CAFE
THE **WEIRDEST** THING HAPPENED.
WHAT?

I FOUND MY SCIENCE REPORT. IT WAS AT **HOME.**
YEAH?

THE ONE YOU FOUND IN MY **LOCKER.**

WHAT ARE YOU SAYING?
sup Ruth
FREE

I'M SAYING THERE WERE **TWO** OF THEM!
OH.
LOST: my dignity
JUICE

DO
YOU...

DO YOU MIND IF I SIT WITH YOU? I THINK MADISON...
OF COURSE!

SO, NO REACTION TO ME HAVING TWO SCIENCE REPORTS?

DID YOU PRINT IT OUT TWICE?

I **REALLY** DON'T THINK I DID.
WHY LOOK A GIFT HORSE IN THE MOUTH?

YOU READY FOR ANOTHER **MAGE PROPHECY** BEATDOWN, THOMAS ELFKIN OF THE GLADE?
Juice

ONE SEC, ELDER MATT. I'M APPARENTLY LOSING MY MIND.

...MAYBE IT WAS **MAGIC.**

I'M BEING SERIOUS.
IT'S PROBABLY THE NSA. THEY PROBABLY FELT BAD FOR ME.

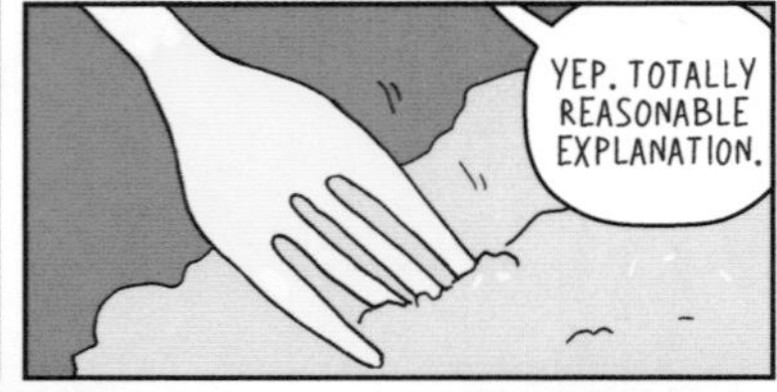
YEP. TOTALLY REASONABLE EXPLANATION.

THAT'S ENOUGH ***FLIRTING***, TOMMY. YOU OWE ME A **MAGE PROPHECY** BATTLE.
sigh

W-WE'RE NOT FLIRTING!
what mean flirt?

FINE. RANDALL AND I CAN PLAY.
WHAT AM I, CHOPPED LIVER?

DID YOU NOTICE WE'RE, LIKE, THE ONLY SUNNYSIDERS IN CLUSTER 3?

AMANDA IS A SUNNYSIDER. SHE'S PRETTY COOL.
I WENT TO SUNNYSIDE.

AMANDA HAS...

...BEHAVIORAL ISSUES.
STAB
STAB
KILL

JOAN AND LEAH ARE BOTH IN CLUSTER 1. THEY'RE OUT THERE, HAVING FUN TOGETHER, LEAVING ME IN THE CLUSTER 3 DUST.

I THOUGHT YOU WERE LIKE, BEST FRIENDS WITH THE NEW GIRL... MADISON, RIGHT?
...

THINGS ARE... WEIRD WITH HER.

AND EVERYONE ELSE IN MY CLASSES IS *FROM* MOHICAN ELEMENTARY.
YEAH, ALL THE MOHICAN KIDS KNOW EACH OTHER ALREADY.

I DIDN'T REALLY HAVE A LOT OF *FRIENDS* AT SUNNYSIDE, EITHER, SO IT'S ALL THE SAME TO ME.

ROCK LEGEND
CAFE
Danburg

JOAN AND LEAH AND I WERE PRETTY MEAN TO YOU AT SUNNYSIDE, WEREN'T WE.

I GUESS.

WE BOOED YOU AT THE SPEECH FESTIVAL.
That was you?

I'LL BE IN THERAPY FOR LIFE FROM THAT. THANKS.

I WAS SUCH A LITTLE TURD. I THINK I WAS JUST TRYING TO RAISE MY OWN SOCIAL STANDING.
LOOKS LIKE IT WORKED GREAT FOR YOU. HERE YOU ARE, AT THE **MAGE PROPHECY** TABLE.

ACK!

HEY, DUDE.

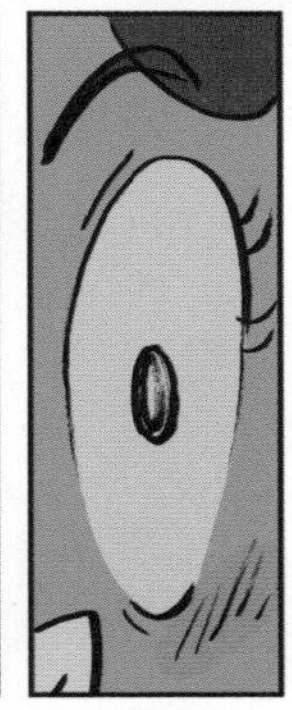

OH NO, YOU'RE NOT **FRIENDS** WITH HIM, ARE--
?

CAREFUL, TOM!

YOU'LL CATCH HER **UGLY!**

THIS IS KARMA. FOR THE **SPEECH FESTIVAL.**

YOU'RE NOT SUPPOSED TO MAKE GIRLS CRY!
?

PUSH!
Kill him
Tears of the innocent

OW!

GUESS I HAVE "BEHAVIORAL ISSUES," TOO.
SUNNYSIDERS STAND TOGETHER!
DRAG
Live often Laugh hard Love much
Modular Sofas Warehouse
CLEARANCE (caution: haunted)
$500

you can tell me anything!
NO ONE CAN MAKE YOU FEEL INFERIOR WITHOUT YOUR CONSENT
-Eleanor Roosevelt
you let this happen
GUIDANCE

TOM WAS JUST STICKING UP FOR ME. NICK IS THE **REAL** VILLAIN IN THIS SITUATION.
**NO** I'M NOT! I'M THE **VICTIM!**

**NICK** IS ALWAYS SAYING REALLY MEAN THINGS TO ME. HE IS ABSOLUTELY **RUINING** MY LIFE.
NICK CALLED ME **"DANIEL,"** HE SAID I WAS **FAT**, AND HE SAID HE'D RATHER DATE KEVIN THAN ME, **AND** HE SAID TOM WOULD CATCH MY **UGLY**--
I HAVE MORE, IF I CAN CONSULT MY DIARY--

WE TAKE BULLYING VERY SERIOUSLY, NICK.

B-BUT I GOT PUSHED! I'M THE VICTIM!
OW
DON'T YOU KNOW HOW BULLYING WORKS?!

TOM MADE AN ERROR IN JUDGMENT. HE WAS BEING CHIVALROUS, THOUGH.

ARE YOU GOING TO TELL OUR PARENTS?

CRAP
WE ALREADY CALLED ALL YOUR PARENTS. IT'S SCHOOL POLICY.

I KNOW SEVENTH GRADE IS TOUGH. SO I'LL GO EASY ON YOU-- BUT NO MORE FIGHTING, OKAY?
I DIDN'T DO ANY FIGHTING. I WAS THE VICTIM.

YEAH, I GOT IT, NICK.

YOU'LL ALL WATCH AN ANTI-BULLYING VIDEO, AND TOM AND NICK WILL HAVE AFTER-SCHOOL DETENTION.
GUIDAN

I DON'T THINK *I* NEED TO WATCH THE VIDEO.
I ALREADY HAVE **PLENTY** OF FIRSTHAND EXPERIENCE FROM **NICK.**

I DON'T KNOW WHY YOU KIDS THINK YOU HAVE ANY BARGAINING POWER IN THIS SITUATION.

TYPE
TYPE

anti bullying psa
YOO TOOB
Recommended
10 hours of MEDITATION
40,000 plays
Everyone Hates Her!
GOTH

STUPID 90S PSA
BULLYING Hurts Feelings
WITH MC DONALD
CLOWN BAGS
KID FALLING FAIL
GUI

BULLYING: DON'T DO IT!
BULLYING: HURTS FEELINGS!

HEY, I'M LEGALLY OBLIGATED TO APPEAR
IN THIS VIDEO, BUT I WANT YOU TO HEAR
A LITTLE STORY 'BOUT HOW FEELINGS ARE HURT--

WHEN YOU MAKE YOUR PEERS FEEL LIKE DIRT!
?!

BULLYING: DON'T DO IT!
BULLYING: HURTS FEELINGS!

THAT WAS VERY ENLIGHTENING.
I'LL NEVER BULLY AGAIN.
HURTS FEELINGS!
Need to talk?
See your Guidance Counse
301

AHH
whoa!
STORM

HEY, NICK, THAT WASN'T VERY NICE! **HURTS FEELINGS!**
hee hee

.......

ha
ha
ha

HAHAAA... OH MAN, MY PARENTS ARE **LITERALLY** GOING TO MURDER ME.
LITERALLY?

THEY'RE GOING TO SMOTHER ME WITH A PILLOW WHILE I SLEEP. I'M NOT LOOKING FORWARD TO IT.
I HEARD THAT'S ONE OF THE NICER WAYS TO GO. PEACEFULLY, IN YOUR SLEEP, SURROUNDED BY LOVED ONES.
GYM
BEST EFFORT
#3!
MAINE

...NOW MY PARENTS ARE GONNA KNOW I'M A LOSER. SIGH.
HALL PASS
Name: Dana Something
Period:
Signature:
CAN
DY!

HEY, SHE DIDN'T WRITE THE TIME ON THESE HALL PASSES. WE COULD TOTALLY SKIP PERIOD 5B.
VEND

DITORIUM
PEP RALLY
VEND
I DIDN'T ACTUALLY MANAGE TO EAT MY LUNCH BEFORE ALL THE HUBBUB. DO YOU WANT SOME SNACKS?
YOU'RE EVIL! THE ANTI-BULLYING VIDEO TURNED YOU EVIL!

I DON'T HAVE MONEY. I'M A FREE-LUNCH KID.

I HAVE MONEY. I HAVE TONS OF MONEY.
...
LET'S
CHEPS

...CAN I TELL YOU A SECRET? WILL YOU PROMISE TO NOT TELL ANYONE, INCLUDING AND ESPECIALLY GOVERNMENT OFFICIALS?
TURN

Yes.

THIS IS A **MAGIC COIN PURSE.** MONEY JUST COMES OUT OF IT.

HA, HA.

I KID YOU NOT.

AGH! DON'T **DO** THAT! DO YOU WANNA GET **CAUGHT?!**
FSHHHHHHH

LIKE I SAID, DON'T TELL ANYONE ABOUT THIS. IT WOULD PROBABLY START WORLD WAR III.

...THAT MEANS MADISON IS, LIKE, YOUR **IMAGINARY FRIEND?**
SHE'S **REAL!** SHE'S A **REAL PERSON!**
I DON'T KNOW WHY EVERYONE FINDS THAT SO HARD TO GRASP.

BUT THAT'S WHY IT'S AWKWARD.
I THINK SHE RESENTS ME.

THAT'S KIND OF FUNNY, BECAUSE YOU CREATED HER FOR THE SOLE PURPOSE OF LIKING YOU.

ha ha
I GUESS MY TERRIBLE PERSONALITY IS STRONGER THAN MAGIC.

DO YOU HAVE THE NOTEBOOK WITH YOU?
IT'S IN MY LOCKER RIGHT NOW. JUST IN CASE. PRINCE NEPTUNE IS GUARDING IT.
I'VE GOT A SHEET OF SPECIAL PAPER FOR EMERGENCIES, THOUGH.

ALL THE ANIME BABES OUT THERE, AND YOU BRING **PRINCE FREAKIN' NEPTUNE** INTO EXISTENCE.

WHOA. YOU COULD, LIKE, SOLVE WORLD HUNGER. STOP WARS.

YEAH, BUT DIDN'T YOU SEE THAT EPISODE OF ***Z-FILES*** WHERE HE TRIES TO SOLVE THOSE THINGS AND IT MAKES HUMANITY DISAPPEAR?

...FAIR ENOUGH.

I DON'T EVEN KNOW HOW TO FIX THE PROBLEM WITH MADISON.
AND I FEEL LIKE I'M JUST WAITING FOR THE OTHER SHOE TO DROP EVERY TIME I DRAW SOMETHING.

WHAT ARE YOU KIDS DOING?!
AHHHHH
SPLSH

HALL PASSES! WE HAVE HALL PASSES!!
HALL PASS
NAME: Dana Something
PERIOD:
SIGNATURE:

HALL PASSES DON'T PERMIT YOU TO HANG OUT IN THE STAIRWELL! GET TO CLASS!!
SCAMPER
SCAMPER

FWOOSH!

Cheltzer
SNACKLES
2 CUPCAKES FAMILY SIZE

...IF THE SCHOOL HEALTH INITIATIVE BOARD COULD SEE THIS...

BRRINGG

GO TEAM

H-HEY, MADISON. HOW'S LIFE?

TERRIBLE.

UM...
DO YOU WANT TO STAY OVER TONIGHT?
OFFICE
I'VE GOT SOMEWHERE TO STAY ALREADY.
IT EVEN HAS A VENDING MACHINE.

ARE YOU STAYING AT THE JOLLY ROGER?
HUH?

OH. THE MOTEL? YEAH, IT'S NOT SO BAD.

JUST...

LET ME HELP YOU? I'VE BEEN THINKING ABOUT IT, AND...

MY PARENTS CAN ADOPT YOU.

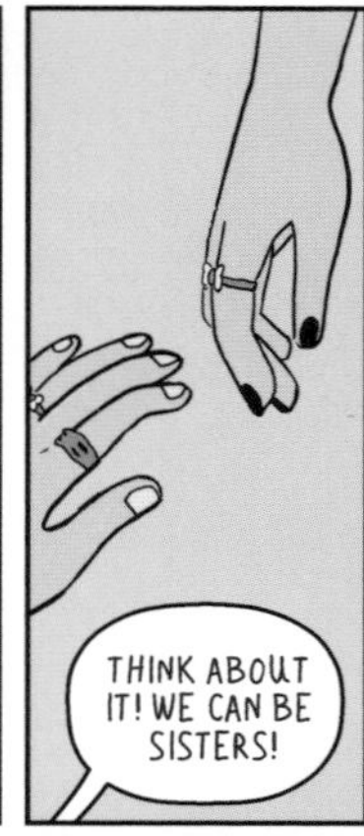
THINK ABOUT IT! WE CAN BE SISTERS!

I CAN TAKE CARE OF MYSELF.
BUS

PLEASE... DON'T WORRY ABOUT ME. I DON'T NEED ANYONE'S PITY.

**MADISON.** YOU DON'T HAVE TO BE ALONE.

LOOK, DANY, I LOVE YOU AND ALL-- BUT I NEED SPACE.
I NEED TO FIGURE OUT WHO I AM.
LIKE, WHO I AM WITHOUT YOU.
...IT'S LIKE I'VE GOT THIS CURSE ON ME, AND IT'S TELLING ME 24/7: "LOOK OUT FOR DANY!"
"BE NICE TO DANY!"
"WOULDN'T THIS BE BETTER IF DANY WERE AROUND?"
AND I DON'T KNOW IF THAT'S BECAUSE I'M PROGRAMMED TO BE YOUR BEST FRIEND,
OR IF IT'S BECAUSE I'M, WHAT, A WEEK OLD AND IMPRINTING ON YOU LIKE A STUPID BABY DUCK.

AWW, BUT BABY DUCKS ARE CUTE!

THAT'S-- THAT'S NOT THE POINT. C'MON.

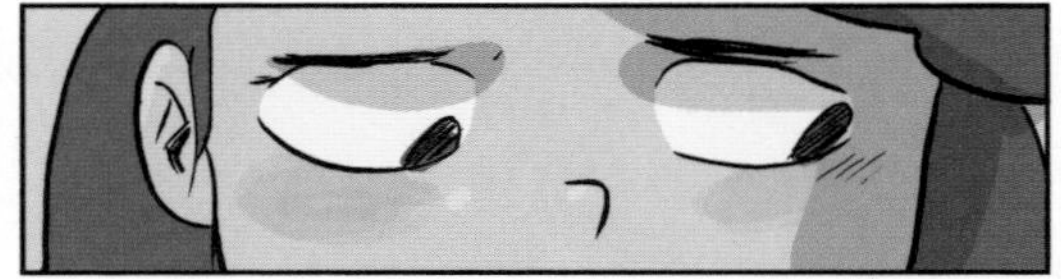

SO...I SHOULD LEAVE YOU ALONE FROM NOW ON.
ROCK LEGEND CAFE DANBURY

I CAN TAKE CARE OF MY OWN PROBLEMS ALL BY MYSELF.
AND I BELIEVE IN YOU...

YOU CAN MAKE FRIENDS THE NORMAL WAY.
B-BUT WHAT BUS ARE YOU TAKING?
ROCK LEGEND
NOT YOURS.
MELTON MIDDLE SCHOOL
ROCK LEGEND CAFE
DANBURY

SCHOOLBUS
VROO

A+E

FLOAT

SO I GUESS I GOTTA MAKE FRIENDS "THE NORMAL WAY."
FLOAT

THROUGH MY PERSONALITY.

ACTUALLY, DEAR PRINCESS DANIELLE, I HAVE A **BETTER** PLAN.
BETTER THAN MY PERSONALITY?

ALTHOUGH YOURS IS TRULY THE MOST **ASTONISHINGLY GLORIOUS** PERSONALITY I'VE EVER HAD THE **PRIVILEGE** OF WITNESSING, **MY** PLAN WILL HAVE YOU AT THE TOP OF THE SOCIAL HIERARCHY IN **MERE DAYS.**

**MERE DAYS,** YOU SAY?
CONSIDER IT A SOCIAL EXPERIMENT.

ONLY-- YOU MUST SWEAR TO FOLLOW MY INSTRUCTIONS TO THE **LETTER.**
YOU GOT IT.

blah blah Madison

YOU WANNA SLEEP OVER TONIGHT? MY PARENTS ARE AWAY AGAIN.
AND THE HOUSE GETS KINDA SPOOKY WHEN I'M ALONE.
TOTALLY!
DON'T YOU HAVE TO CHECK WITH YOUR PARENTS?
NAH.

COOL.
hah
TRAITOROUS GIRL.

I'M GLAD MADISON IS STAYING WITH CARA. IT'S NOT LIKE I OWN HER.

ALSO, CARA'S THE COOLEST GIRL IN CLUSTER 3. WHO **WOULDN'T** WANT TO HANG OUT WITH HER OVER ME?

*I* WOULDN'T.

CARA RULES THE SCHOOL. SHE'S LIVING THE DREAM. EVERYONE ALREADY **WANTS** TO BE HER FRIEND.
EXIT

BUT I GUESS I'VE GOTTA MAKE FRIENDS THE OLD-FASHIONED WAY:
EXIT
TEXTBOOKS a history

BY SITTING QUIETLY UNTIL SOMEONE NOTICES ME.

DANY!! GUESS WHAT!!
AP's

TOM! HI!

LOOK WHAT I GOT WITH YOUR MONEY.
BATTLEMAN
RONALD

THE **BATTLEMAN X** MANGA. IT'S EVEN GORIER THAN THE SHOW.
**WOW!**

SAY "BATTLEMAN X IS STUPID."

I READ THESE ONES ALREADY. YOU'RE GONNA GET A KICK OUT OF THEM.
DANIELLE? IS THIS THING WORKING?
AW, COOL! EW!! EYEBALLS!!

**BATTLEMAN X** IS STUPID. DON'T ASSOCIATE YOURSELF WITH THIS SOCIAL PARIAH.
STOP IT!!

YOU KNOW, THEY HAD A LOT OF COOL MANGA I'D NEVER EVEN **HEARD** OF AT THE STORE.
AP's Ghostly Writings

YEAH?

MAYBE WE CAN CHECK IT OUT SOMETIME.

THAT... COULD BE FUN? BYE?
SCAMPER
bye

THIS BOY DOES **NOT** IMPRESS ME.
ESPAÑOL

***TOM?*** TOM'S NOT SO BAD! YOU'VE JUST GOTTA GIVE HIM A CHANCE.
SPORTS!

AND I CAN'T SAY **BATTLEMAN X** IS STUPID! IT'S MY THIRD FAVORITE SHOW ***OF ALL TIME!***
I CRIED SO MUCH WHEN BOKU FELL INTO THE TIME-PIT TRYING TO SAVE HAMMY—

MY LOVELY PRINCESS DANIELLE. **SO** PASSIONATE.
BUT **POPULAR** GIRLS DON'T **WATCH BATTLEMAN X.**
"A real page-turner!" -Pythagoras
AND THEY ALSO DON'T TALK TO THEMSELVES **QUITE** SO LOUDLY.
OOPS.
AMERICA
god bless

CRAZY GIRL TALKING TO HERSELF. WHERE'S YOUR CRAZY FRIEND TO DEFEND YOU?

KLUNK
I'M NOT CRAZY! I'M REHEARSING LINES FOR A P--
I MEAN--

NICK, YOU FOOL NO ONE WITH YOUR BRAGGADOCIO.

WE ALL SEE THE WEAK LITTLE WORM YOU TRULY ARE.
AMERICA
god bless

WAIT for it...

NO ONE LIKES YOU.

NICE IMPROVISATION!
hyuck hyuck
I'll get you Daniel

...AND, LIKE, WHY DO WE HAVE TO LEARN ABOUT THESE OLD DEAD PEOPLE?

HOW DOES IT HELP **ANYONE** TO READ TEN WHOLE PAGES ABOUT THE **COTTON GIN**?
ha ha

I'D LIKE TO GET THOSE PRECIOUS MINUTES OF MY **DWINDLING CHILDHOOD** BACK, THANKS.

ELI WHITNEY WAS A NOTABLE CONNECTICUT RESIDENT! HE CHANGED THE--
Mrs. Marks
Thomas Edison
cotton gin

THE--
I CAN'T BELIEVE SHE REALLY DID IT.
HUH?

CARA MADE ME SWITCH SEATS WITH MADISON. I REALLY...
THOUGHT WE WERE FRIENDS.

SAY: "CLEARLY CARA LIKES SPENDING TIME WITH MADISON. IT MAKES SENSE TO ME."
wat

no no no

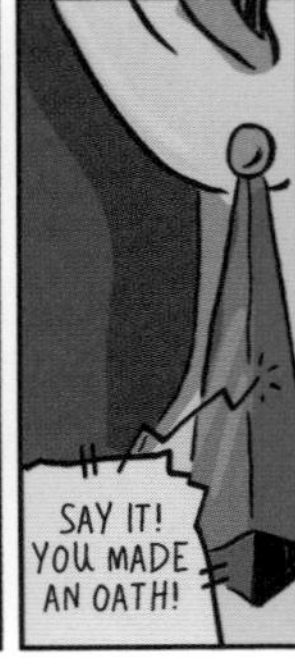
SAY IT! YOU MADE AN OATH!

CLEARLY CARA LIKES SPENDING TIME WITH MADISON. IT MAKES SENSE TO ME.
WIPE!

BUT SHE USED TO **LIKE** TO SPEND TIME WITH ME!
DO YOU KNOW HOW LONG WE'VE BEEN BEST FRIENDS? SINCE, LIKE, **KINDERGARTEN!**

"MAYBE SHE'S BORED OF YOU."

M-MAYBE SHE'S BORED OF YOU.

AM I... BORING?

LAUGH AND SAY, "JUST A LITTLE."

HA, HA. JUST A LITTLE.

I JUST CAN'T DO THIS-- I'M--

I'M KIDDING! YOU'RE **REALLY** INTERESTING. **I** LIKE YOU.
YOU'RE GREAT!

ALL MY HARD WORK!
DANIELLE-- IF YOU WANT YOUR CLASSMATES TO RESPECT YOU, JUST FOLLOW MY COMMAND!

you doing okay there?
BUT I DON'T WANT TO BE MEAN.

ME NEITHER, BUT IF I'M BEING HONEST-- CARA IS **NOT** AS COOL AS SHE THINKS SHE IS.

ISN'T HOW COOL YOU ARE MEASURED BY HOW MUCH YOU DON'T CARE?

THAT'S WHAT... **MADISON** TOLD ME.

I'M JUST SAYING, AND WE'RE ALL THINKING IT: THE INDUSTRIAL REVOLUTION IS KINDA OVERHYPED.

WELL, I HAVE **ALL** THE DIRT ON CARA. SEVEN YEARS' WORTH.

SHE **DEFINITELY** CARES WHAT PEOPLE THINK.
HERSTORY
MAGELLAN
HA
HA
HA
ha
ha
ha
Blah blah blah

**MADISON FONTAINE!** IF YOU DON'T STOP **INTERRUPTING** MY **CLASS**, I'LL HAVE TO MAKE A CALL TO YOUR **PARENTS!**
GOOD LUCK.

**THAT'S IT.** GATHER YOUR BELONGINGS. YOU'RE GOING TO THE OFFICE. **NOW.**

WOO!
WOO!
We the people
Mrs. Marks
History is important
ELI WHITNEY MATTERED
YEAH!
WOOHOOO
CLAP CLAP
BOISTEROUS APPROVAL
CLAP CLAP
WOOOO
CLAP CLAP

WOO

...YEAH, I'VE BEEN WRITING AN OBOE CONCERTO IN MY SPARE TIME. BUT I'M STUCK ON ONE PART.
LAUGH TO YOURSELF.

HA HA HA.
UM, WHAT'S SO FUNNY?

...NOTHING.
GREAT JOB, THAT WAS PERFECT.

WHEN DID YOU START PLAYING THE OBOE?
I STARTED WHEN I WAS LIKE...FIVE?

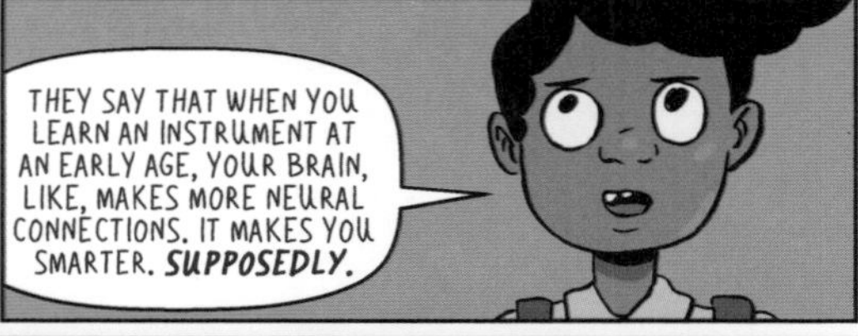
THEY SAY THAT WHEN YOU LEARN AN INSTRUMENT AT AN EARLY AGE, YOUR BRAIN, LIKE, MAKES MORE NEURAL CONNECTIONS. IT MAKES YOU SMARTER. SUPPOSEDLY.

MY PARENTS ARE LIKE, SOOO INTO THAT KIND OF STUFF. IT GETS ANNOYING.
sigh

SAY:
"YOU SAY 'LIKE' A LOT. I THOUGHT YOU WERE ONE OF THE **SMART** HUMANS."

YOU SAY "LIKE" A LOT. I THOUGHT YOU... WERE...

***EXCUSE*** ME?

IT'S A SIGN OF LOW INTELLIGENCE.
IT'S A SIGN OF...LOW INTELLIGENCE?

...

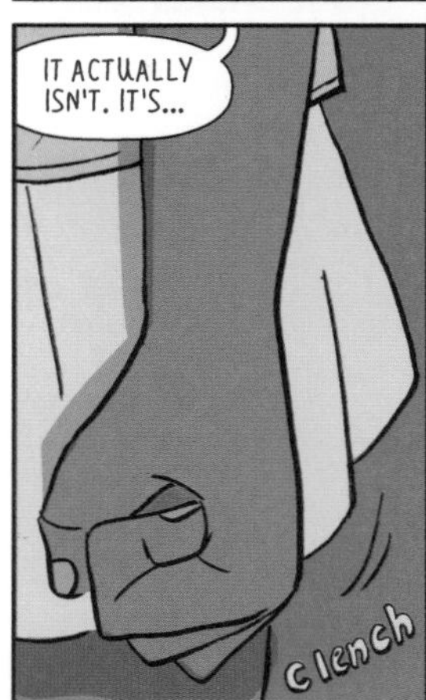
IT ACTUALLY ISN'T. IT'S...
clench

...I DON'T NEED TO EXPLAIN IT TO YOU. **BYE.**
no!
sniff sniff

ALEESHA! WAIT!!

PRINCESS DANIELLE, HOW **COULD**--
YOU'RE RUINING MY LIFE

I-- I DIDN'T...

MEAN IT...

WHATEVER. I DON'T CARE WHAT ANYONE THINKS OF ME.
sniff

I WAS TRYING TO BE COOL, SO I SAID MEAN STUFF.

YOU'RE LIKE, THE SMARTEST KID IN CLUSTER 3.

YOU SAY "LIKE," TOO!
IT'S SUCH A USEFUL WORD.

**MY** MOM SAYS IT'S **ELITIST** TO POLICE PEOPLE'S SPEECH PATTERNS.
Yeah..?

YOU CAN STOP APOLOGIZING ALREADY. GIVE ME YOUR NEWTFLAX PASSWORD AND WE'LL CALL IT EVEN.
LIFE
SUX
SCIENCE
FROGS
OKAY!

IT'S "PASSWORD."
You don't need to write it down...
SKRIT!

THANKS. I COULD USE SOMETHING TO WATCH WHILE I'M PRACTICING SCALES.

Conjugar verbos
AR-
ER-
IR

ESPERO MEJOR DE TI, SEÑOR TORRES.
Tom Torres
85
Escriba algo.
yo quiero mas helado
Me llamo Tomás Torr
¿Donde esta la tie
Escuchar
Mi sueño en la vida es encontrar unos extra terrestr

85

WHAT DID SHE JUST SAY?
SHE... HOPES FOR MORE OF ME?

**EW,** IS MRS. ESPOSITO ***HITTING ON YOU?***
hee hee!
En un lugar de la Mancha

NO, I COMPLETELY BOMBED THE QUIZ.

AND I GUESS I'M SUPPOSED TO SPEAK SPANISH ALREADY AND GET STRAIGHT A'S.

WHY DON'T YOU? AREN'T YOU FROM MEXICO?
MY MOM ***TRIES*** TO TEACH ME.

I CAN'T REMEMBER WHERE THE ACCENTS GO.

ANYWAY, MY **FAMILY** IS GUATEMALAN, BUT **I'M** AN AMERICAN.

**YOU'RE** NOT AN AMERICAN.

READ AN ATLAS, **NICK**; GUATEMALA IS PART OF CENTRAL **AMERICA** AND THEREFORE TECHNICALLY GUATEMALANS **ARE** AMERICANS.
NO, I MEAN I'M A U.S. CITIZEN...

SEÑORA ESPOSITO, **TOM** HAS AN ADVANTAGE. IT'S NOT **FAIR.**

SHUT UP, STUPID!
¡EN ESPAÑOL!

UM...
¡CÁLLATE, ESTÚPIDO!

BIEN DICHO, SEÑOR TORRES.
¿Y NICK? ¿TU RESPUESTA?
VERBOS
SUSTANTIV
CONJUGAR

NO ES **FAIR!** NO ME GUSTA!!
KRRR-R-R

SCHOOL SPIRIT

brr!
SWW

...pep rally this afternoon...
YAY
MMs

**...ALEESHA'S** MISSING CLASS, DOING BAND STUFF FOR THE PEP RALLY.
I HAVE NO ONE TO TALK TO.

IT'S LIKE IT WAS BEFORE MADISON, ALL OVER AGAIN.
I'M ALL ALONE.

IF YOU'D ACTUALLY FOLLOW MY DIRECTIONS, YOU WOULD ALREADY BE POPULAR WITH EVERYONE, NOT JUST THE REJECTS.

CALL ME CRAZY, BUT I DON'T THINK PEOPLE LIKE IT WHEN YOU JUST WALK UP TO THEM AND INSULT THEM.
Does that girl EVER stop talking to her locker?

DO YOU KNOW WHAT HAPPENS WHEN YOU LET OTHERS IN?
WHEN YOU SPEAK THE TRUTH OF YOUR SOUL?

Friendship?

...YOU HAND THEM YOUR POWER. YOU BECOME WEAK.

FRIENDSHIP IS **DEPENDENCY.**
uh...

LOOK, I **GET** IT.
WHATEVER KIND OF **LESSON** YOU'RE TRYING TO TEACH ME BY **DESTROYING** MY **SOCIAL LIFE**–

"BULLYING IS **BAD**!"
"POPULARITY ISN'T IMPORTANT!"
"**REAL** FRIENDS LIKE THE **REAL** YOU–"

I THINK I'VE **TRULY LEARNED** SOMETHING FROM OUR LITTLE EXPERIMENT.

MY GENTLE, EARNEST PRINCESS, YOUR RECITAL OF CHEAP BROMIDES PROVES YOU HAVE **LEARNED NOTHING.**
SLUMP
wha?
BUT I UNDERSTAND.

YOU...
YOU DON'T **TRUST** ME. YOU BELIEVE ME TO BE BEYOND **REDEMPTION.**

AFTER ALL, IF YOU BELIEVE YOU HAVE "NO ONE TO TALK TO," THEN I MUST NOT BE OF MUCH VALUE TO YOU.
WAIT... I DIDN'T MEAN IT LIKE THAT!

I COULD HAVE BECOME YOUR CLASSMATE, LIKE MADISON.

BUT YOU KEEP ME CAGED. BODILESS.

AND, FORBIDDEN MY PRIMARY SOURCE OF SUSTENANCE, **HUMAN ENERGY**, IMMENSELY WEAKENED.

I'M...
I'M SORRY!! DO YOU NEED HUMAN ENERGY? YOU CAN TAKE SOME OF MINE!

FWOO
I DON'T CARE, IT'S...TOTALLY FINE...WITH...ME!

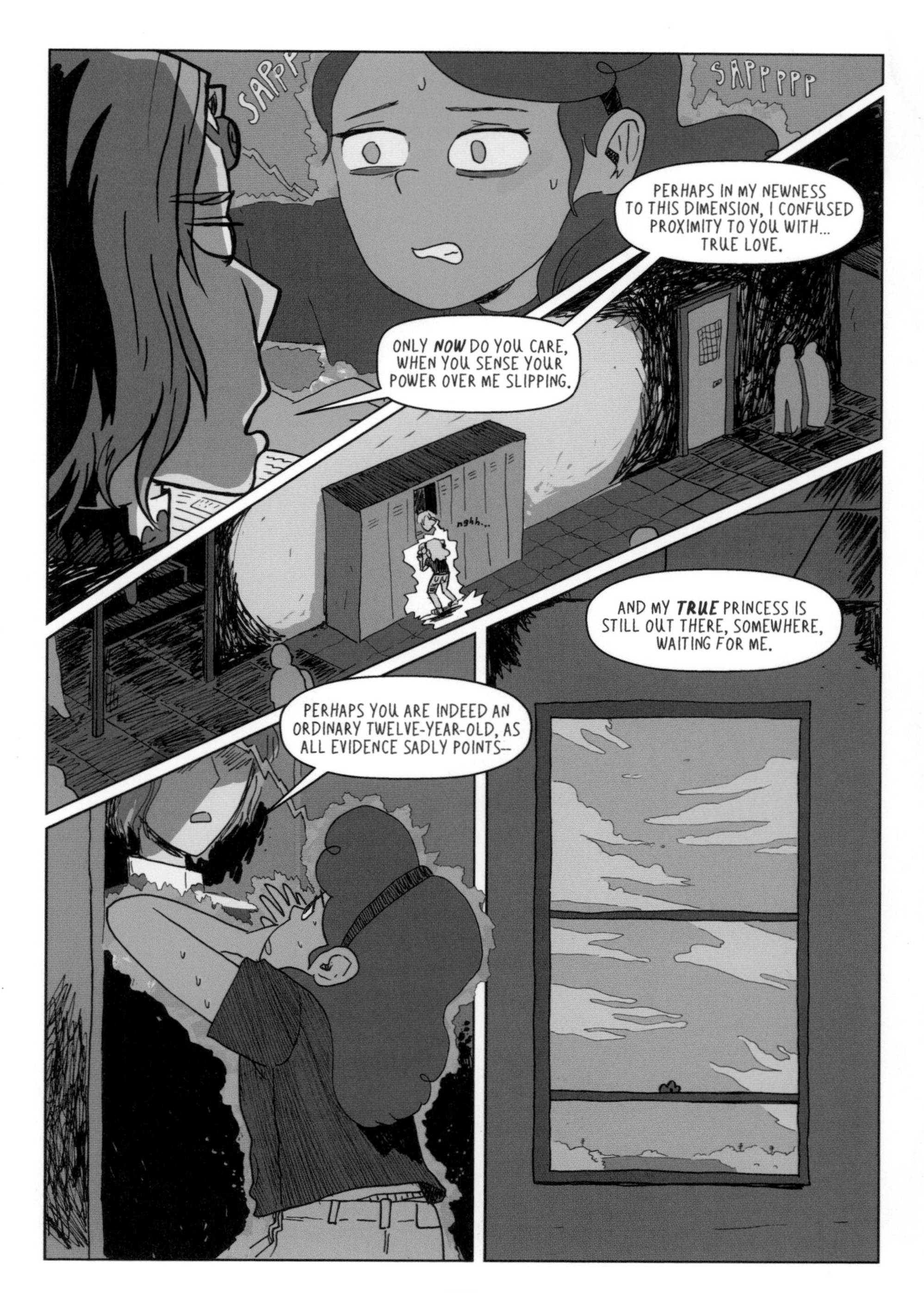
SAPP
SAPPPPP
PERHAPS IN MY NEWNESS TO THIS DIMENSION, I CONFUSED PROXIMITY TO YOU WITH... TRUE LOVE.
ONLY **NOW** DO YOU CARE, WHEN YOU SENSE YOUR POWER OVER ME SLIPPING.
nghh...
AND MY **TRUE** PRINCESS IS STILL OUT THERE, SOMEWHERE, WAITING FOR ME.
PERHAPS YOU ARE INDEED AN ORDINARY TWELVE-YEAR-OLD, AS ALL EVIDENCE SADLY POINTS--

YOU'RE JUST LIKE ALL THE REST. JUST LIKE SOLAR RAE.
YOU DON'T PLACE VALUE IN THE GRANDEUR OF MY PLANS, ONLY IN THE TRIVIAL FEELINGS OF YOUR CLASSMATES.
CEASE
SAP

CLASSMATES WHO WOULDN'T NOTICE IF YOU DISAPPEARED COMPLETELY.
urgh...

RALL PEPPY
WHEREAS I WOULD SIT IN THIS DANK CELL ALL DAY FOR THE OPPORTUNITY TO JUST...

...BE NEAR YOU.

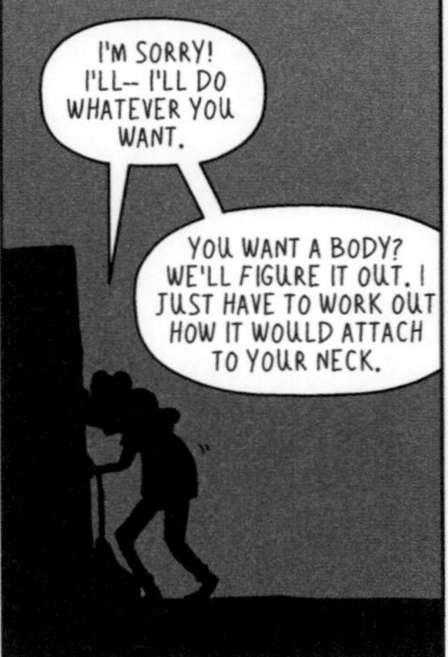
I'M SORRY! I'LL-- I'LL DO WHATEVER YOU WANT.
YOU WANT A BODY? WE'LL FIGURE IT OUT. I JUST HAVE TO WORK OUT HOW IT WOULD ATTACH TO YOUR NECK.

I CAN ASK MY SCIENCE TEACHER HOW NECKS WORK.

NEPTUNE?

I'M...

I'M SORRY.

GET OFF THE FLOOR! GET TO CLASS!
five more minutes...

...HER? REALLY?

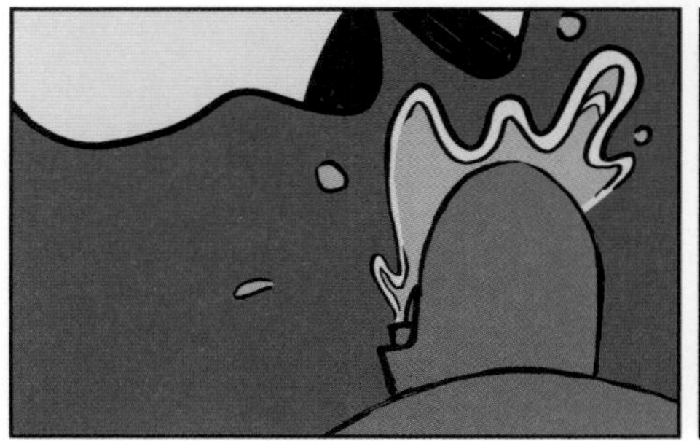

STUDENT ART
H-HI, AMANDA.

DO I KNOW YOU?
WIPE

I THINK WE WENT TO SUNNYSIDE TOGETHER.
ARE YOU OKAY?

YOU'RE COMING ACROSS WEAK!

...?
I'M FINE... HOW ARE YOU?
FINE.

"YOU REALLY LIKE WEARING THAT SHIRT, DON'T YOU."
Sigh

GLANCE

SO WHAT?

"YOU'D BE PRETTY WITHOUT ALL THAT RACCOON EYE MAKEUP."
Seriously?

ARE WE FRIENDS NOW?

COOL! YOU WANNA EXCHANGE--
heh

WIELD!
S-SOCIAL MEDIA INFORMATION?!

STAB!! STAB

AAAHHHHHHHH

AAAAAHHHHHH

STAB

STAB

STAB

STAB

STAB

STAB

WHAT'S HAPPENING? YOU'RE BLOCKING THE CAMERA!

STAB
STAB
STAB
STAB
STAB
STAB
AHHHHHH
CRASH
YOU STAY AWAY FROM HER.
YOU DON'T TELL ME WHAT TO DO.
GRAB
OR I TELL SKYE AND REX ABOUT THIS. WE CLEAR?
BUNCHA WEIRDOS.
huff

DANY!
watch it!
whaa...?
PUSH

ARE YOU OKAY?
I THINK SHE JUST KINDA...

DREW ON MY ARMS. BUT HARD.

I GUESS THE PEN ISN'T MIGHTIER THAN THE SWORD, AFTER ALL.
GOOD THING SHE LEFT HER SWORD AT HOME TODAY!

heh
heh
heh

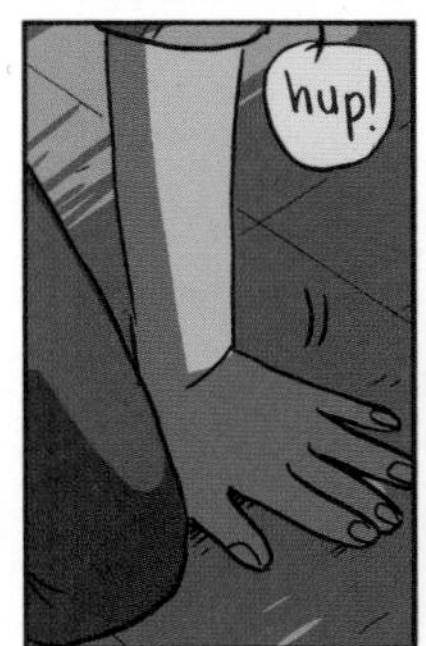
hup!

I'M FINE, NOT THAT YOU CARE--
sorry
huff!

OKAY, WELL, SEE YA, DANY.

MADISON! W-WAIT!

M-Madison... Uh... Thanks...
?

THANKS... FOR PROTECTING ME.
YOU KINDA BROKE OUR LITTLE AGREEMENT.

OH, DANY...

WHY THE **HECK** WOULD YOU BULLY **AMANDA?** SHE'S HAD A TOUGH LIFE, YOU KNOW. SHE'S NOT OKAY.
UM, WELL, PRINCE NEPTUNE IS TRYING TO HELP ME MAKE FRIENDS.

HE TELLS ME WHAT TO SAY THROUGH THESE MAGIC **EARRINGS.**
!

NEPTUNE, YOU **IDIOT!**
IF YOU **CARED** ABOUT DANY **AT ALL,** YOU WOULDN'T PUT HER IN DANGER! WHAT IS **WRONG** WITH YOU?! YOU SHOULD BE **PROTECTING** HER!
GRAB

MY POOR EARS!!

GIVE ME THE EARRINGS.

SQUEAK
SQUEAK
CRANK
CRANK

TOSS!

I'VE BEEN WORRIED SICK ABOUT YOU!
meh
I'M FINE, I'M FINE! **SHEESH!**
ARE YOU STILL LIVING AT THE JOLLY ROGER?
HUH?
YOU SAID YOU WERE STAYING THERE.
?
YOU SAID IT HAD A GOOD VENDING MACHINE...?
**HAH!** OH, DANY...

JOLLY ROGER
MOTEL
IT WAS NOTHING AS FANCY AS A MOTEL.

ROOMS AVAILABLE eminently habitable
MUST BE OVER 18 WITH VALID ID
Courtesy is Contagious
I TRIED, BUT EVEN WITH MY FAT STACKS OF CASH, THE MOTEL SAID THEY COULDN'T RENT A ROOM TO A MINOR.

I COULD'VE MADE YOU A FAKE ID!
IT'S FINE.
JOLLY ROGER
MOTEL

WOL·MORT
never too much
ENTER
SALE
CLOSED
I HAD A PRETTY GENIUS BACKUP PLAN, IF I DO SAY SO MYSELF.

slide

security cam 4000
snip!

Child Labor™
brand
Maternity Dresses
LOW PRICES
$7

MOTOR
OIL
CHEESEBURG-O's

JUMP!
SILLY SLIDES

FWOOOSH
my best friend
She likes what you like
I like bananas!
I LIKE IT TOO
CALL 1-800-MYBESTFRAND
CALL
TV!
SALE!

ChildLabor™
brand
Baby Plushies
LOW PRICES
$5
meal-n-a-BAG
NOT MY CHILD

Primordial Coo
CRIME STREETS
Minako
31
友だち
K.O.
demo
DISCOUNT BIN
YEAH, I JUST CAMPED OUT AT WOLMORT, LIVING THE PERFECT VAGRANT LIFE.
Meal-n-a-BAG
Tilapia casserole
CLICK
CLICK

UNTIL MRS. MARKS-- MORE LIKE MRS. NARCS, BECAUSE SHE NARCED ME OUT-- FOUND OUT ABOUT MY LACK OF PARENTS AND HOME ADDRESS.
CLICK
CLICK

come back
REAL

WE'LL FIND AND PROSECUTE THE LIVING HECK OUT OF YOUR FOLKS.
CTHULU BURGER
HEY KID!
AHOY!

IT JUST AIN'T RIGHT TO ABANDON YOUR KID.
nom nom

I DON'T MIND LIVING IN WOLMORT.
I THINK WOLMORT MINDS, KID.

THEY ALREADY FOUND ME A FOSTER FAMILY...

HAVE A
DAY
AT LEAST FOR NOW.

SO I GUESS I WENT FROM HAVING NO FAMILY TO HAVING A **LOT** OF FAMILY.
my new family
INCLUDING **AMANDA,** WEIRDLY ENOUGH.
I GUESS YOU DIDN'T KNOW THAT SHE'S A FOSTER KID.
TABITHA
SAD DEATH

YEAH, IT JUST KINDA FIGURED ITSELF OUT.
LIFE'S FUNNY LIKE THAT, HUH?
omg....

YOU COULD'VE GOTTEN MURDERED. I SHOULD HAVE BEEN THERE WITH YOU... TO HELP YOU...

YOU WOULDA JUST GOTTEN MURDERED RIGHT ALONGSIDE ME.
THAT'S WHAT FRIENDS ARE FOR!
B12 ENERG

THE MELTON MIDDLE SCHOOL PEP RALLY STARTS IN FIFTEEN MINUTES! EVERYONE, PLEASE HEAD TO THE GYM TO CHEER ON THE WILD BEARS!

UGH, A PEP RALLY? **REALLY?**
**HEH.** I JOINED **CHEERLEADING,** ACTUALLY.

I LIKE THE OUTFIT.
YOU **DID?!**

THAT'S... COOL.
GOOD FOR EXTRACURRICULARS AND STUFF.

YEAH. OKAY, I GOTTA GO! WISH ME LUCK!
got book?

GOOD LUCK!

GO TEAM
MELTON WILD BEARS
BEAR DOWN
for game day!

OH, THANK **GOD.** JOAN AND LEAH.

HEY! GUYS! LEAH TUNG & JOAN QUINCY! over hereeee
WAVE
BOING
Dany!!

MELTON PROUD
PEP
EXIT

RHONDA!!

DANIELLE, RHONDA. RHONDA, DANIELLE.
POINT!

I SAW YOUR ARM DRAWINGS! THEY'RE **AWESOME!**
YEAH, I LOVE TO DRAW.

DRAW ON HER ARM!
OK!
DO IT!!

I'M GONNA BE A TATTOO ARTIST WHEN I GROW UP.
100 colorful GEL PENS

MY PARENTS WON'T LET ME GET ANY INK YET, THOUGH.

BEARS are STRONGER than DOGS!
Sorry, Bridgeford, it's SCIENCE
GO WILD BEARS!
DON'T YOU HAVE TO BE **EIGHTEEN** TO GET A TATTOO?
THAT'S WHAT THEY SAY. IT'S SO UNFAIR!

...DID SOMEONE ALREADY DRAW ALL OVER YOUR ARMS?
HEH, YEAH, I GOT STABBED WITH A PEN.

WOW, CLUSTER 3 IS **INTENSE.**

HEY! ALEESHA!

GUYS, THIS IS ALEESHA. SHE'S A MASTER OBOIST.
#3
1994
YAY

I NEVER SAID **THAT.**
heh...

BUT, UH, HI?

I LIKE YOUR HAT.
...

wave
HISS!
EW, **TOM,** GO AWAY!

THIS IS A
BOY-FREE
ZONE.

never
mind...
TURN

NO, NO,
HE'S COOL.

heh
it was no
biggie
TOM BEAT UP
NICK MALONEY
FOR ME.

GASP!
WHAT?!

...WHO'S NICK
MALONEY?
NO CLUE.

...YEAH, DURING
LUNCH LAST WEEK.
WE ALL GOT SENT TO
THE OFFICE.
FIRST LUNCH WAVE IS
SO MUCH COOLER THAN
SECOND LUNCH WAVE.

when do we clap?
??

MMS
MMS

MADISON'S A CHEERLEADER NOW?!
SHE'S HER OWN PERSON.

GO MADISON! WOOOOoooo
WOOOO
MADISON'S a CHEERLEADER?!
who?
madison

heh
BRIDGEFORD WON'T KNOW WHAT HAS HIT 'EM
WHEN WE DESTROY THEM ON THE FIELD
MMS
THEIR PARENTS WILL ALL MOURN THEIR CHILDREN
GO MADISON!!
BRAND
SQUEAK
THE EARTH AWASH WITH THEIR TEARS

NOW LOOK AT THAT **SCHOOL SPIRIT.** WE'RE GONNA DO **GREAT** AT THE **GAME** TONIGHT!
NOW LET'S WELCOME THE **MELTON MIDDLE SCHOOL** BA--
KRRRRR
BZZZT!!
CRACK!
GO TEAM
CHAMP 1998
MMS

RRRR
RUN!
RIIPPPP
TEAMWORK
FWO
STAY CALM! WE NEED EVERYONE TO PROCEED IN AN ORDERLY FASHION OUT OF THE GYMNASIUM—
EXIT

CLICK!
NO ONE IS LEAVING JUST YET.
WHERE IS PRINCESS DANIELLE?
who?
um
P-PRINCE NEPTUNE COSPLAYER?
it's CANON?!
help
HE'S beautiful
AHH
how is he flying
AHH
MAGIC is REAL!

OKAY, GUYS, NO TIME TO EXPLAIN. I MAY HAVE MISTAKENLY BROUGHT PRINCE NEPTUNE TO LIFE.
outta my way!!
BUT... JUST HIS HEAD. I DON'T KNOW WHERE HE GOT THE BODY.
SKRTCH
UM.
WE'VE GOT TO SAVE THE SCHOOL!! OKAY?!
WE'RE ALL GOING TO DIE! WHY ARE YOU DRAWING?
omg
you like to draw too?
FOUR MAGIC FLYING RINGS, JUST LIKE MINE.
POOF
FIVE SOLAR SISTERS™ TRANSFORMATION LOCKETS.
POWER UP, GUYS.
POOF
DRAW

HEY!
C'MON, YOU ALL GOTTA EVACUATE! THIS IS SERIOUS!

TAKE THESE!
THE FATE OF THE SCHOOL DEPENDS ON IT!
HUH?
OMG
DO I GET ONE?

THE RING WILL LET YOU FLY. THE OTHER THING IS...
what is going ON

SOLAR SISTERS TRANSFORMATION LOCKETS?!

WHAT AM I SUPPOSED TO DO WITH THESE?
EXIT
This is definitely Dany's fault
PUT THEM ON! WE'VE GOT TO FIGHT PRINCE NEPTUNE!
UH, CAN I JUST WATCH YOU GUYS FIGHT PRINCE NEPTUNE? I HAVE ASTHMA.
SAPPP
AHH! YOUR HUMAN ENERGY IS SO DELICIOUS!
SAPPPPP

ELDER MATT!!
By the rays of the sun, TRANSFORM!

POSE!
By the rays of the sun, TRANSFORM!
THIS WON'T GIVE ME A SOLAR SISTERS UNIFORM, WILL IT?
WELL... UH...
"BY THE RAYS OF THE SUN, TRANSFORM!"
EVERYONE LOOK AWAY!

By the rays of the sun, TRANSFORM!
UM... "By the rays of the sun, TRANSFORM"?
I KNOW WE'RE ABOUT TO DIE, BUT I JUST GOTTA SAY--
THIS IS THE GREATEST MOMENT OF MY LIFE!
DING!

PRINCE NEPTUNE! STOP THIS TERROR AT ONCE!
THERE YOU ARE, MY LOVELY PRINCESS DANIELLE.
SAPP
AND YET... YOU DON THE GARB OF MY NEMESES, THE **SOLAR SISTERS**?
hey it's the girl who talks to her locker
FWOOOO
WHAT?!
FWOOOO
Dany!

FWOOOO
OOOOOO
Lengthen
Prin cess Form
Fwooo
HOW MANY MAKEOVERS DOES DANY NEED?!
Dany's evolving!!
THAT'S BETTER.

ooh....

um

PRINCE NEPTUNE! YOU CAN'T DO THIS!

PRINCESS DANIELLE... I'M TAKING OVER THIS LAND OF CONNECTICUT FOR YOU.
EXIT

I REALIZE NOW-- I CAN'T MAKE YOU POPULAR.

IT'S A LITERAL IMPOSSIBILITY.
...

YOU WILL NEVER, EVER BE POPULAR.
OKAY, I GET THE POINT!

BUT I CAN MAKE YOU POWERFUL! FEARED!
WHICH IS FAR SUPERIOR, IN MY OWN EXPERIENCE.

LOOK AT THESE FOOLISH, FRIGHTENED CHILDREN, WHOSE APPROVAL YOU SO DESPERATELY CRAVE.
EXIT

THEY'RE JUST PEOPLE.
DOESN'T IT SEEM SO SILLY NOW TO FEAR THEM?

NO MORE QUIBBLING, MY DEAR. I SHALL TAKE THIS LAND OF CONNECTICUT IN YOUR NAME.
A PRINCESS NEEDS HER KINGDOM.

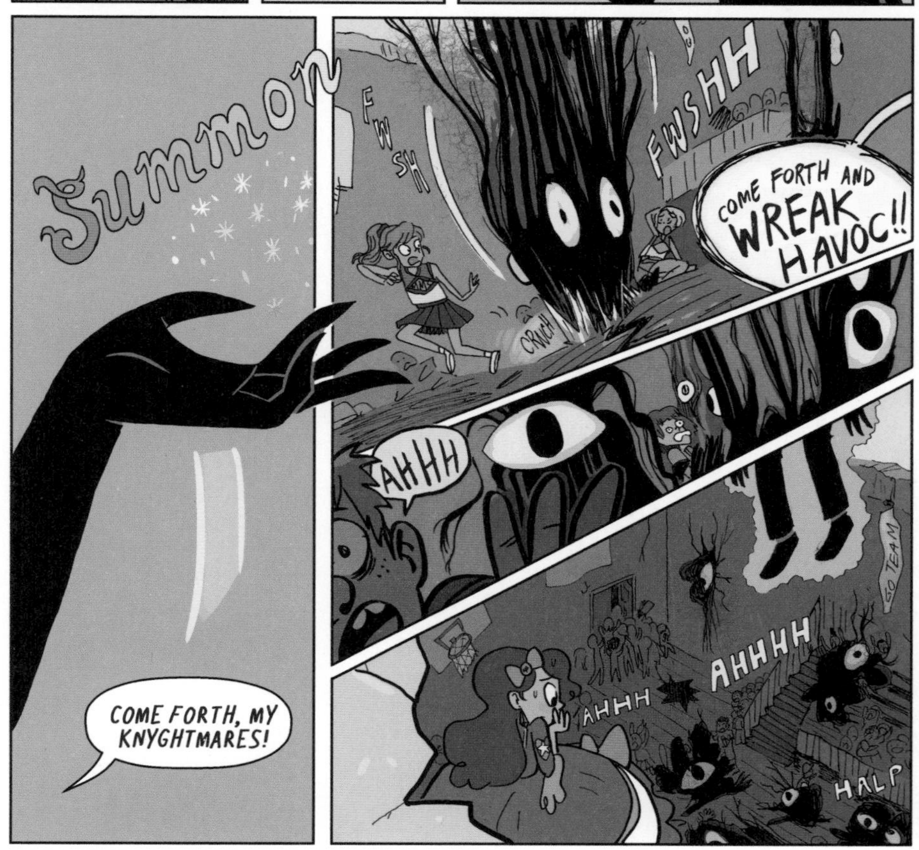
Summon
COME FORTH, MY KNYGHTMARES!
FWSH
FWSHH
COME FORTH AND WREAK HAVOC!!
CRUNCH
AHHH
GO TEAM
AHHHH
AHHH
HALP

TO ALL YOU FOUL CRETINS IN THIS CESSPOOL OF PUBLIC EDUCATION:
YOU MUST NEVER TORMENT PRINCESS DANIELLE AGAIN!
NO BULLYING!
GO TEAM
School Spirit
AHH
AHH
who?!!
DANIEL THE MANIEL IS IN AN UGLY FRILLY DRESS!
HAHAHA!
STOP IT, THAT'S SO EMBARRASSING!
KICK
THIS DRESS IS LOVELY!

ONLY A FOUL **PIG** WOULD SAY SUCH THINGS ABOUT THE MOST **WONDERFUL** GIRL, THE **PRINCESS** OF THIS REALM.
DUDE, SHE'S **NOT** A PRINCESS--
FWOOOOO
POOF!
SQUEEEALL
heh heh, classic... now change him back...
Never.
PRINCE NEPTUNE! PLEASE! STOP HURTING MY CLASSMATES!
YOU CAN'T JUST— SURE, NICK MALONEY'S A TOTAL **JERK.** AND HE'S GOT A BAD 'TUDE.
B-BUT MORTAL ENEMY OR NOT, NO ONE DESERVES SUCH CRUEL AND UNUSUAL **PUNISHMENT**! CHANGE HIM **BACK**!

No.
Uh... how do my powers work
Um...
SOLAR FLARE!
GO
Rmble..
DODGE
CRACK!

NEED REINFORCEMENTS?
yay
WOBBLE
SOLAR PUNCH!
KAPOW
WHAM!
PROPERTY DAMAGE!
FWOOSH!
Whoops...

grr...

Nothing personal, dude...

WAIT, WE CAN FLY?
Did I mention I'm AFRAID OF HEIGHTS?!

APPARENTLY!
...I DON'T KNOW WHAT MY POWER INCANTATION IS.

I JUST MADE UP SOLAR PUNCH.

SOLAR PUNCH TOTALLY SHOULD'VE BEEN MY MOVE.

OOH! I GOT IT!

TRUTH BOMB!

BURN!
YOU'RE A MINOR CHARACTER ♥
BOOM!
ZING
UM, IF WE'RE REALLY GOING TO BATTLE THE...
FOOLISH HUMAN.
keff keff
(I CARRIED season 2!)
EVIL PRINCE FROM SOLAR SISTERS ...

LET'S AT LEAST KEEP THE STUDENTS AND TEACHERS OUT OF IT.
SOLAR PUNCH!
?!!
PULL!
TRUTHBOMB!
YOU'RE GROSS
BOOM

HAH! YOU'LL NEVER DEFEAT ME!
SAPPP

GOOD THINKING, LEAH!
TO THE FOOTBALL FIELD!
Ahhhh....
Wobble
wobble
I'M GONNA DIE!!!!!

OUR FATHER, WHO ART IN HEAVEN--

GRAB!

YOU'RE NOT GONNA DIE! YOU ARE IN CONTROL.

YOU CAN DO THIS.
WE'RE NOT EVEN THAT HIGH UP!

JUST DON'T LOOK--

LOOK

LURCH

Down
hyugh

**LEAH!** USE YOUR **SOLAR POWERS** TO HELP YOU!
AHHHHHHH
NEPTUNE! THIS HAS GOT TO END!
GOOD IDEA...
The Knyghtmares are back!!
FWOOSH!
FWOOSH
SLAPP
ZAPPP
this is bad

ZZAPPPPPuuuuuuuhh
S-solar... urghhh... helppp
zzZAPPP!!
IT'S LIKE POKING AN ELECTRIC SOCKET WITH A FORK...
ZAPPPPP
I DON'T KNOW WHY YOU CARE SO MUCH ABOUT THOSE MISERABLE **HUMANS,** PRINCESS DANIELLE.

I DON'T PARTICULARLY LIKE MOST OF THEM, BUT HUMAN LIFE HAS VALUE!
YES, IT DOES HAVE VALUE. IT'S DELICIOUS.
I'LL DO MORE WITH THOSE HUMANS' LIFE ENERGY THAN THEY COULD EVER DREAM OF DOING!
I'LL TURN THIS WHOLE PLANET INTO OUR KINGDOM!
ZAPPPP

WE'LL RULE THIS BEAUTIFUL PLANET! WE'LL STOP THE SUFFERING AND WAR AND HUNGER—

N-NEVER!

DID YOU JUST SAY "NEVER" TO STOPPING WAR AND HUNGER?
GEEZ, DANIELLE. THAT'S HARSH.
ZAP
TH-THAT CAME OUT WRONG!

WELL, WE DON'T **HAVE** TO STOP SUFFERING AND WAR AND HUNGER IF YOU DON'T **WANT** TO.
IT WAS JUST A SUGGESTION.
ZAPPA
WE CAN DO ANYTHING. WITH THIS BOOK--
MY SKETCHBOOK!
YES. BAD IDEA TO LEAVE ME ALONE WITH IT.
IT WAS REALLY CRAMPED IN THAT LOCKER. WHAT A LOGISTICAL NIGHTMARE.
FWOO
HOW DID HE DRAW WITHOUT ARMS?
ZZAPP
HE HAS TELEKINESIS!

NO MATTER. WITH MY HORDES OF **KNYGHTMARES**, MY BOUNDLESS **HUMAN ENERGY SOURCE**, AND MY **PRINCESS** AT MY SIDE--
WE WILL CHANGE THE WORLD!
ZZAPPPP

!
FWSH!

FLICK
is it over? did I die? g'night

MADISON?
Solar Punch!

FIRST YOU BETRAY PRINCESS DANIELLE, AND NOW ME.
I SHOULDN'T BE SURPRISED-- AND YET... I'D BELIEVED US TO BE FRIENDS, AT ONE TIME.
FWOOSH

"FRIENDS" DON'T TAKE OVER YOUR WORLD.

IT'S NOT REALLY YOUR WORLD, THOUGH, IS IT?
SIZZZ...
FLIP
RIP!!
DANY, CATCH!
TOSS
M-Madison?
THANKS!
ATTACK, KNYGHTMARES!

ANIMAL PAL! I SUMMON THEE!
CHAOS ARPEGGIATING!
CHOMP
BOOM
RIP THE PAPER! MAYBE THAT'LL BREAK THE SPELL!
FWIP!

LAAAAAAAAAAAAAAAAH!!
DON'T!!
MADISON! YOU'RE ON THE OTHER SIDE OF THE PAPER!
NO HARD FEELINGS

I'VE HAD A GOOD RUN. THANKS FOR EVERYTHING, DANY.

LIFE REALLY IS SOMETHIN' ELSE.

KRRR!!
MS

NOOOOOO!

MADISON!

YOU CAN'T JUST THROW YOUR LIFE AWAY!

IT DOESN'T MATTER HOW YOU CAME INTO EXISTENCE. YOU'RE ALIVE, JUST LIKE EVERYONE ELSE. YOU'RE NOT, LIKE, EXPENDABLE.

AND YOU. PRINCE NEPTUNE.
YOU CLAIM TO "CARE" ABOUT ME. DO YOU REALLY THINK I WANT MY TOWN TO GET DESTROYED?! MY CLASSMATES TO GET ATTACKED?!

YOU SAID YOU WERE GOOD. THAT THE SOLAR SISTERS MANGA WAS AN UNFAIR PORTRAYAL.

BUT LOOK AT WHAT YOU'RE DOING.

YOU NEED A KINGDOM--
NO ONE HAS KINGDOMS HERE.
IT'S 'MURICA!
WE HAVE ELECTED OFFICIALS HERE. IT'S NOT PERFECT, BUT AT LEAST WE GET TO TRY AGAIN EVERY FEW YEARS.
I DON'T WANT TO BE A PRINCESS.
hee hee
I'LL BE A PRINCESS!
THEN WHY DID YOU EVEN BRING ME INTO EXISTENCE?

IT WAS AN ACCIDENT. I WAS JUST DRAWING A PICTURE.

I... UNDERSTAND, PRINCESS DANIELLE.
JUST REGULAR DANIELLE.

I UNDERSTAND, "REGULAR DANIELLE." I AM NOT MEANT FOR THIS WORLD.

kiss♡

OMG

UM... WHY ARE THEY MAKING OUT?
DOES THIS MEAN THE FIGHT'S OVER?
C'mon, Dany... show some judgment...
YOINK!
...AND SO, I WILL **RESHAPE** THIS WORLD TO FIT MY NEEDS!
WOOSH
WAIT, **WHAT?!**

COME ON, NEPTUNE.
YOU HAD A **CLEAR** OPENING TO TAKE THE HIGH ROAD--
WALK AWAY FROM ALL THIS WHILE KEEPING **SOME** SENSE OF GOODNESS.
THE HIGH ROAD IS OVERRATED. BUT YOU'RE ALWAYS WELCOME TO RULE MY NEW WORLD AT MY SIDE, **REGULAR DANIELLE.**

NOT A CHANCE!

I'VE GOT A PLAN, EVERYONE!
WE'LL VANQUISH HIM WITH...

THE POWER OF **FRIENDSHIP!**

GUYS?

I- I HEARD YOU, DANY. THE POWER OF FRIENDSHIP.

HOW DO YOU WEAPONIZE FRIENDSHIP?

EVERYONE! HOLD HANDS!

PAH! THE POWER OF FRIENDSHIP? WHAT NONSENSE! THAT'S NOT REAL POWER.
NOT LIKE... BECOMING RULER OF CONNECTICUT!
AND SOON, THE ENTIRE TRI-STATE AREA!
DUDE, THIS IS HOW LIKE EVERY SEASON OF **SOLAR SISTERS** ENDS!
MADISON! WE NEED YOU!
BUT... I DON'T HAVE A **SOLAR SISTERS'** LOCKET...

YOU'RE MADE OF MAGIC! AND FRIENDSHIP!
M.M.S
K.O.!
FRIENDSHIP FEELS... ALL TINGLY...
FWOOO
FWOOO

FWOOo°
PRINCE NEPTUNE! I HEREBY BANISH YOU!
FWOOOOOo°
FWOOoo
MMS
TO THE MOON!
YEAH, TO THE MOON!
AND...

... STAY THERE!
Take me with you
Adiós muchacho

watch it, bud!
FWOOSH!!
INTERNET
ON

WEE
OOO
WEE
OOO
WE

WELP.
WE BROKE THE SCHOOL.
WE'RE **SO** DEAD.
ESPECIALLY DANY.
WEE
OOO
WEE
OOO

I GUESS I **SHOULD** WATCH MORE TV. I DIDN'T UNDERSTAND **ANY** OF WHAT JUST HAPPENED.

LIKE, CAN THAT MAN SURVIVE THE RADIATION IN THE EARTH'S ATMOSPHERE?

WHO CARES? YOU STILL KICKED BUTT!
PAT

I OUGHTA **SUE** THE SCHOOL FOR NEGLIGENCE.

THE ROOF WAS **CLEARLY** NOT UP TO CODE-- ANY **ONE** OF YOU KIDS COULD'VE DIED!
TRAITOR JOE
I survived the MELTON
BUNS

...SUE THEM UNTIL THERE **IS** NO MORE SCHOOL.
is that supposed to be a good thing?

LUCKY. YOU GET TO MISS SCHOOL.
JUST A WEEK OR TWO. WE GOT A CALL FROM THE SCHOOL BOARD.
ALL THE KIDS ARE GETTING SHIPPED OFF TO OTHER SCHOOLS IN THE DISTRICT.
...YOU KNOW, THIS IS WHY I ALWAYS HATED THIS SCHOOL DISTRICT.
THE PEOPLE WHO RUN IT ARE IDIOTS.

WHAT.

MAYBE WE'LL GET THE SAME SCHOOL.

IT'S JUST UNTIL THEY'RE DONE WITH REPAIRS.
I'M SO WORRIED THIS WILL RUIN YOUR EDUCATIONS.

HA, HA, DANY, YOU'RE GONNA BE DUMB FOREVER!
...

SWEET! THAT MEANS MY SCIENCE TEST IS CANCELED! I'LL NEVER HAVE TO FIND OUT WHAT A SWIM BLADDER DOES!

THE SWIM BLADDER HELPS A FISH MAINTAIN ITS LEVEL OF BUOYANCY.

NOOO... THE EDUCATION, IT HURTS!
ha ha
I survived the MELTON METEOR!

clink

SO. I KIND OF HAD A KAMIKAZE FREAK-OUT TODAY, DIDN'T I.
KAMIKAZE FREAK-OUT WOULD BE A REALLY GOOD BAND NAME.
IT WOULD BE. AND YEAH, YOU DID.

BUT AT LEAST NOW YOU KNOW-- LIKE, SERIOUSLY, YOU DEFINITELY KNOW--
YOU'RE A PERSON, A REAL HUMAN PERSON.

YEAH, I GOT IT. I'M REAL.
...AND I'M SORRY I'VE BEEN STANDOFFISH LATELY.
BUT AT LEAST THAT PROVES I REALLY DO HAVE FREE WILL.
I Survived the MELTON METEOR

OTHERWISE YOU WOULD HAVE BEEN MAGICALLY COMPELLED TO KEEP HANGING OUT WITH ME!
YEAH!

Y-YOU'RE NOT BEING MAGICALLY COMPELLED TO HANG OUT WITH ME RIGHT NOW, ARE YOU?
NO...?
I CAUSED the MELTON

AWESOME!

WE CAN'T JUST PLAY WITH MAGIC LIKE IT'S SOME TOY.
WE'VE GOT **SUPERPOWERS.** WE SHOULD USE THEM TO, LIKE, MAKE A DIFFERENCE.
CHANGE THE WORLD. **RESHAPE** IT. MAKE IT **BETTER.**
WE COULD DESIGN **UTOPIA.**
BUT WE DON'T KNOW IF MAGIC HAS, LIKE...
JOG

..."SIDE EFFECTS"...

WELL, I'LL DESIGN A UTOPIA ANYWAY, JUST IN CASE WE EVER NEED ONE.

*I* THINK WE SHOULD TELL A GROWN-UP ABOUT ALL THIS. I'M SORRY, DANY, BUT I DON'T TRUST YOU WITH LIMITLESS POWER...

DANY WOULDN'T BETRAY US!
haha
I don't trust you with magic either
heh
**LEAH!** YOU WOULD TRUST A **GROWN-UP?!**

GROWN-UPS ARE ACTIVELY RUINING THE WORLD.
CAN YOU IMAGINE HOW MUCH **FASTER** THEY'D RUIN IT IF THEY HAD MAGIC?
WE SHOULD USE OUR SUPERPOWERS TO FIGHT CRIME AND END INJUSTICE!

I'M ALL FOR CRIME-FIGHTING, B-BUT... UM ... AM I THE THE ONLY ONE GOING TO BRIDGEFORD MIDDLE SCHOOL?

PITY
aw...

JK lol everything's fine guys
JOG

CAN'T YOU USE **MAGIC** TO CHANGE THE ASSIGNMENT?

IT'S JUST A MONTH. YOU CAN DO IT!

DON'T WORRY, WE **ALL** PROMISE NOT TO HAVE FUN WITHOUT YOU.
r-really?
no

BUT I WON'T HAVE MY WINGMAN!
WING-**GIRL.**

HEH. I'M GONNA BE COMPLETELY FRIENDLESS AGAIN.
JOG

YOU'LL MAKE FRIENDS. ***I*** BELIEVE IN YOU.

DON'T THINK ABOUT IT SO MUCH! IT'S JUST **RANDOM!** FRIENDS JUST **HAPPEN!**
MAYBE TO **YOU.**
WHEN **I** DIDN'T HAVE FRIENDS, I JUST FOCUSED ON LEVELING UP MY **PIKKIMALS.**
NOW I HAVE A LEVEL 100 CHANSARD. AND NO ONE CAN TAKE THAT FROM ME.

WOULD YOU TRADE IT FOR A HOLOGRAPHIC LEVEL 82 **ROCKABABY?**
ARE YOU-- SHE'S MY **STARTER** PIKKIMAL! **NEVER!**

IT'S REALLY NOT THAT HARD TO MAKE FRIENDS.
JUST ASK PEOPLE ABOUT THEMSELVES. PEOPLE LOVE TALKING ABOUT THEMSELVES.
WE LOVE THE SOUND OF OUR OWN VOICES.

HA! I'M GONNA TRY THAT ONE OUT!
JOAN, WHAT'S YOUR FAVORITE COLOR?
RAINBOW!
WOW

...ISN'T ANYONE GOING TO ASK **ME** HOW TO MAKE FRIENDS?

AWW, SORRY! WHAT DO YOU RECOMMEND, LEAH?
ha ha

JUST...DON'T BE SO WRAPPED UP IN YOURSELF, DANY. GET OUT OF YOUR HEAD A LITTLE!
AND NEXT TIME YOU'RE IN TROUBLE, LET US IN. **WE'RE** YOUR FRIENDS. **ALREADY.**
...FRANKLY, I'M OFFENDED YOU DIDN'T TELL ME YOU WERE GETTING BULLIED. I'VE KNOWN YOU SINCE BEFORE YOU WERE POTTY-TRAINED.

SORRY...
JOG

WE LOVE YOU AND WE ALL KNEW YOU WERE A DORK ALREADY.
got it...

CLASS SCHEDULE

*Melton Meteor Kids Program*
Danielle Radley

Period 1: Math/Krzowski 210b
Period 2: Spanish/Caporale 301
Period 3: Language Arts/Tolstoy Jr.
Period 4: Managing your personal brand/Delmo 102

YOU'RE IN MY FIRST PERIOD!
I'M SO SORRY. MR. KRZOWSKI IS A VERY BITTER MAN.

IT'S THIS WAY. WERE YOU THERE WHEN THE GYM COLLAPSED?!
IT WAS DURING THE PEP RALLY. PRETTY SCARY.

EVERYONE SAYS YOU GUYS DID IT SO YOU WOULDN'T HAVE TO FACE US AT FOOTBALL.
YOU'VE STUMBLED UPON OUR SECRET! PLEASE, DON'T TELL THE INSURANCE COMPANY!

THINGS AREN'T AS CRAZY HERE, THOUGH. IT'S KINDA LAME.
I'M FINE WITH A BIT LESS CRAZINESS! JUST TELL ME EVERYTHING I NEED TO KNOW ABOUT BRIDGEFORD.

WELL! THE FIRST THING IS, DON'T BELIEVE THE EIGHTH GRADERS; THERE'S NO POOL ON THE ROOF. OH, ALSO...

WHAT THE--?! VARMINTS!
Squeee!

USE MAIN ENTRANCE

FIELD

SQUEEE!

oink oink

NICK MALONEY? IS THAT YOU?!

I WONDERED WHAT HAPPENED TO YOU. I THOUGHT THE SPELL WOULD HAVE WORN OFF BY NOW.
YOU REALLY WERE VERY MEAN TO ME. AT LEAST AS A PIG YOU CAN'T MAKE MY LIFE A NIGHTMARE.
WELL, ALL RIGHT.
JUST REMEMBER: "BULLYING: DON'T DO IT. BULLYING: HURTS FEELINGS."
Sigh.
By the rays of the sun, TRANSFORM!

UH...
SOLAR HEALING POWER?
Reborn!
YOU... SAVED... ME!
YEAH, I KNOW, I'M PRETTY GREAT.
tremble

crap I'm late

...DORK.

FIELD

DASH!

...you basically just run in circles...
blah
blah
huff
huff

...

HEY! NEW KID!
random girl from before (...Emily? Grace!)

RELIEF
GRACE! YOU'RE IN MY GYM CLASS!

LOOKS LIKE IT! MEET MY BESTIES, ROSE AND SOPHIE.

DANY'S FROM MELTON. SHE WAS IN THE GYM WHEN IT GOT HIT BY THAT METEOR.
OH MY GOD! WHAT WAS IT LIKE?
IT...IT WAS LIKE...THE ROOF OPENED UP, AND EVERYONE WAS SCREAMING. PRETTY FREAKY.
FREAKENSTEIN!
huff
huff
shrug

NOW, DON'T START THAT AGAIN...
ha
ha
ha
?
ha
ha
ha

ha ha

YOUR HAIR IS **SO** LONG, DANY. I WISH *I* COULD PULL THAT OFF.

I CAN'T REALLY TAKE ANY CREDIT; IT GREW ALL ON ITS OWN.
huff
ROCK LEGEND

UH, SO, HAVE YOU GUYS KNOWN EACH OTHER LONG?

ROSE AND I MET IN FOURTH GRADE, BUT SOPHIE AND ROSE WENT TO SUMMER CAMP--
IT WASN'T SUMMER CAMP, IT WAS **THEATER CAMP!**
WE DID **LES SAD!**

WHO DID YOU PLAY?
huff
huff

I WAS FATIMA.
I WAS OLD HAG. IT WAS AMAZING.

"GIMME YER HAIR, IT'LL GROW BACK INNA WHILE!"
WOW
"I MUST! IF ONLY TO SAVE MY BELOVED CHILD!"

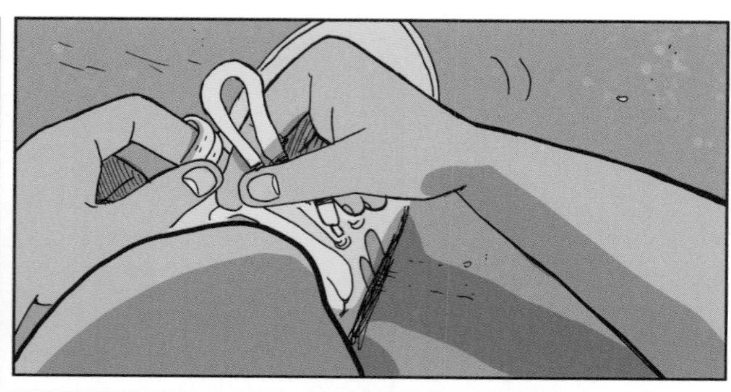

IT'S IMPORTANT TO SING WHILE YOU RUN TO BUILD YOUR VOIIIICEEEE!
SHOW-OFF!
huff
huff

hoo boy

ha ha ha ha
ugh...

SPRINT

omg
Ha HA

ha ha
ha ha
ha ha
ha ha

Hi, everyone! Thanks for reading

# MAKiNG FRiENDS

Here are some extra gags that didn't make it into the book.

Enjoy!

"...Well, it works on MY world..."

## Locker Girl

## Sorry, Rhonda

A NOTE FROM

# KRISTEN GUDSNUK